MW00936459

I

AM

¢URRENCY

Whitney L. Grady

Amazing Things Press

Copyright © 2014 and 2015 by Whitney L. Grady

All rights reserved. No part of this book may be transmitted or reproduced in any form by any means without written permission from the publisher.

Book design by Julie L. Casey
Cover design by Natalia Nesterova and David M. F. Powers

This book is a work of fiction. Any names, characters, or incidents are the product of the author's imagination and are used fictitiously. Any resemblance to actual events, locales, or persons, living or dead is purely coincidental.

ISBN 978-0692496299
Printed in the United States of America.

For more information, visit
www.amazingthingspress.com

For Thomas and Eliza
Dream big

April 19, 2023

The U.S. National Aeronautics and Space Administration, the European Space Agency, the China National Space Administration, and the Australian Government Space Protocol all predict that a meteor will strike the Earth in the next 48 hours. The meteor's projected path has turned and is expected to strike the South Atlantic Ocean near the continent of South America. The people of South America should expect tsunamis and should seek high ground immediately. Across the globe, we may experience earthquakes, flooding, and/or wildfires. Due to the threats, it is recommended that people remain vigilant over the next 48 hours.

The expected strike zone area is a known weak zone in the Earth's magnetic field (known as the South Atlantic Anomaly, an area which has been weakening magnetically for over 400 years). On impact, the magnetic core could be affected, throwing the Earth's magnetic field off balance. Citizens need not worry about the planet's position in the solar system or protection from solar radiation and solar storms, but may experience temporary interruptions in electricity.

More info to come as we follow the development.

WORLD SAFETY COMMISSION
Public Notice

May 1, 2023

In order to maintain a sovereign nation in this post-technological era, the collection of information is an imminent necessity. All citizens are required by law to turn in any existing books immediately to local authorities. Failure to do so by May 5 will result in disciplinary action.

Henceforth, April 21 will be a national holiday when every citizen will be awarded a 10-minute timeslot to privately view specific sections of the library. Note taking will be granted.

1

Red

Quinn's cry echoed across the dry canyon, raising the blond hairs on Nevel's forearms. His heart thrust itself against the walls of his chest as he crouched, waiting to make his next move. This wasn't the first time he had been afraid for his life. He had been scared before: scared for his parents in their dealings with the underground book movement; scared for himself as he held tight to a secret that made him a traitor to the country he loved; scared for the people of this world since the MegaCrash.

Nevel retreated into his mind in search of a specific title to help him in this situation. It was his personal library, shelved with thousands of books. He could see himself enter the imaginary room through a heavy twelve-foot mahogany door, which was covered in an intricate carving showing the story of Persephone and the changing of the seasons.

"NEVEL!"

Beyond the door, richly dark wood shelves stuffed with books reached at least forty feet from the wide-planked cherry floors to a stained glass dome ceiling. Nevel had seen this library on television as a child before the MegaCrash and had never forgotten it. He imagined it was the library of a prestigious college in Europe or perhaps America: the kind of iconic library where attorneys and authors, linguists, and world leaders had studied in quiet solitude deep into the night; the kind of library that demanded respect just by its sheer grandeur; the kind that housed rare books that would require identification to peruse and gloves to handle. The books in this library, however, were all his.

Nevel reached out to run his fingers along their spines, feeling every bumpy binding and embossed letter beneath his fingertips. Within the hard covers, many books were old with thin, crinkly pages and gold edging, while some were newer and full of graphics—all were treasures to Nevel, and he knew them all by heart and more. Calmer now, he focused, searching for the source he was sure existed in the tomes. In his mind, Nevel pulled a book on bats. Flipping to the exact page he had sought, Nevel found what he was looking for.

Fact: Bats use echolocation to determine distance. They send out beeps and listen for variations in the echoes that bounce back at them to determine their distance from other objects or animals.

A cockatoo screeched in the distance. Nevel opened his eyes and wiped at the bead of sweat that had trickled down his temple. He didn't want to send out sounds like the bats to determine his distance from Quinn; he would let the cockatoo do it for him.

He thought he could see the bird's white feathers through the twisted branches of the mulga tree a stone's throw ahead. The bird screeched again, this time lifting into the air, soaring towards the blue sky. The cockatoo's call was definitely closer than that of his name being called in the distance just moments ago. If he had to guess, he'd say that Quinn was at least a mile behind him now, but he was no bat.

He waited a moment to make sure he was about to continue to run away from Quinn and not towards her. His stance was becoming shaky. Shifting his weight from his left leg to his right eased the numbness caused by his crouching stance. The red gravel crunched beneath his hiking boot. The vein in his neck pulsed with the rapid beating of his heart. Nevel scanned the distance before him and then turned to scan all that lay behind him. From his crouch behind the brush, luck offered him a rare glimpse at the red-haired menace as she crossed an open stretch at least a mile behind him. Her back was to him, her ponytail swinging widely as she moved, and her knife gleaming in the bright sun. Nevel bolted in the other direction.

Nevel ran. Legs pumping, flat palms slicing through the air, Nevel moved swiftly through the outback. The smoldering sun scorched his arms. Sweat dripped in constant trails down his temples, and the

3

salt stung his eyes. He squinted against the glaring light from the torturous sun and the flying dust his running unearthed.

He ran until his thighs burned, and his feet ached, and his heart felt as though it would hammer through his chest. It was eerily quiet apart from his heavy footfalls and heavier heaving breaths. He didn't know how long he'd been running—by the pain in his legs, he guessed it had been about ninety minutes—but he didn't hear his name called again. Scanning his surroundings but finding no sign of Quinn, he cautiously slowed to a walk and then stopped altogether, hands on his knees and head hanging. His panting began to slow. Nevel finally took one long deep breath in and then slowly exhaled. His knees were shaking, and, with a prayer that she was still heading west but too exhausted to even consider continuing on anytime soon, he collapsed to the ground.

Lying there in the rocky underbrush, all he could think about was one thing: where was Quinn? Nevel's mind spun to *The Lord of the Flies.* He was Ralph. He was being hunted by his peers. Or maybe just one peer. Nevel hadn't seen anyone but Quinn since his hasty departure from town yesterday, but that didn't mean Quinn was working alone. For all he knew, Quinn could be a part of a whole group just waiting to turn him in. She could be working for someone; someone like Driscoll, or worse, someone like Carrington. Nevel swallowed hard, his mouth dry, although whether from the hours of running in the outback without water or the sudden wave of dread, he wasn't sure.

Just yesterday, he had been with his peers; perhaps he had finally become their target. Flyers posted all over town had everyone on edge. There was a silent witch-hunt afoot, though no one dared speak of it. *Who among us?* This phrase was surely embedded in everyone's minds and kept lumps in their throats.

Nevel had been sitting in Mrs. Downey's tenth grade class, carving a wallaby into his desk with a penknife while he listened to her chatter on about harvesting honey from beehives. It was a lesson they had been taught before, but everyone else was still furiously scribbling down notes. Quinn sat two rows ahead of him, her hair tied back in that long red ponytail. She was wearing her metal-tipped snakeskin boots again. Quinn was striking—the kind of girl most of the boys at The Queensland School seemed to want. Nevel had seen her around school before, and he had rolled his eyes at those boots on more than one occasion. Only the upper crust of society was fortunate enough to use metal for ornamentation. Nevel's dad owned one pair of steel-toe boots, a safety regulation on construction sites. They had been expensive enough, even though he had bought them used and battered, and they certainly weren't snakeskin. Or pink.

Nevel was forced to crane in an attempt to catch a glimpse of the board beyond Quinn's tall stature and perfect posture. Note taking was an essential part of the role Nevel had to play: a poor bloke starving for info. Even though he didn't need the information he copied from the board, he still had to feign interest in it. What aggravated him almost as much as Red's obstruction of his view was Mrs. Downey's poor illustrations and mislabeling, which didn't match anything he could see in the detailed books on bees in his mind. Mrs. Downey had scribbled a lopsided hive and had swapped the Honey Super for the Queen Excluder as the tenth grade class mimicked her every note. These poor blokes didn't have a chance to harvest with this info, Nevel thought, but kept to himself as he dutifully dipped his quill into ink and began to copy the misshapen drawings and even the mislabeled bees into his ledger. To add fuel to the fire raging in Nevel, Harvesting Class was optional for Quinn's type – surely she had people to do her harvesting for her. Red ought to have been three doors down the hall practicing her grip on a teacup—pinky out—not two rows ahead blocking his view.

As he raged in silence, Nevel caught Randy Thatchburne staring at him like a circling buzzard out of the corner of his eye. Randy was a skinny, knobby-kneed, freckle-faced kid with slick, jet-black hair whom Nevel had been in school with since he could remember. In fact, before the MegaCrash, Randy used to come to school with all sorts of electronics that he said his dad had invented. His kindergarten backpack was always beeping, and at recess the kids all gathered around him to drool over the latest gadget. Randy was a bragger and had, on more than one occasion, told a young Nevel that he could never afford the types of technology his dad was putting out there. After technology was rendered useless by the crash, the Thatchburnes didn't fare much better. Rumor had it they found Randy's dad in the barn with a hole in the head. "Suicide," the rumor mill whispered. Nevel felt almost sorry for Randy, until he saw the hungry look on his face. Nevel tapped at his notes while raising his eyebrows at Randy in an effort to remind Randy to stick to the task at hand. Randy rolled his eyes, but he turned back to his own business.

Quinn was still sitting all prim and proper and in his way. Nevel's desk squeaked as he tried to shift to the left to avoid Red's blockade. Katherine Culpeper looked accusingly at him from behind her jagged chocolate brown fringe. From his desk, Nevel could see her ledger, every detail noted in a neat and organized fashion. If he could see her perfectly printed words, she could see his as well: the doodles, the sloppy handwriting, and the blanks that everyone else had already filled in. Nevel slammed his hand on top of his ledger to cover his markings, and Katherine turned back to her own ledger with a smug look. Great, Nevel thought, I am just inviting everyone today to peg me for the target. Looking back towards the board, all he could see was Quinn. He groaned and picked up his quill.

Nevel sharpened his quill with his penknife and brushed the shards and splinters quickly away with the back of his hand. He looked back to the board, hoping to feign attention for the rest of the hour well enough to throw off Randy and Katherine or anyone else that might suspect him when he saw it. In his haste, he had accidentally sent the tiny bits through the air and onto Quinn's perfect ponytail. As if on cue, Quinn raised her hand to her hair and ran her fingers through it, smoothing out the strands. Nevel had seen her do it a million times, her neatly filed finger-nails sliding between the strands as she cocked her head just slightly to the right. Her slender, porcelain fingers stopped, and then pulled a shard. She paused for a moment, inspecting the bit of quill splinters between her fingers, before dropping them to the floor and returning to her note taking. Just when Nevel thought he was safe, she reached up, tucking a lose strand behind her ear and pulled the shiny red length of her ponytail over her shoulder. Within seconds, she produced another shard. And then another. And another. Nevel tucked his chin to his chest and tried to focus on his notes. His cheeks flushed red and he could feel eyes on him.

It took all of his courage to look up. Her bright green eyes were staring at him intently. Her head was cocked, her fingers pulling again in the long red lock that now lay over her shoulder. Slowly, a tiny smile appeared—just a small upward twitch of the right side of her mouth—but her eyes gleamed. She knew. He held her stare, swallowing hard, until he felt his quill snap between his fingers. When he looked back up, he was surprised to see that Quinn had turned back to her note taking. Nevel carefully grasped the broken tip of his quill and did the same.

The school gong tolled. Nevel heaved a sigh of relief. Weaving in and out of students and ducking open lockers, Nevel maneuvered unnoticed through the school hallway like a dingo in a sheep herd. With a push on the long metal bar, the doors opened to the bright afternoon light. Nevel slid down the rail and landed at the bike rack, where his steel framed bike stood ready and waiting. It didn't look like much, rusted metal with two different tires, but it was sturdy and fast. That was enough for him. Nevel launched onto the broken asphalt road that led home.

The ride home that had long ago been a daily struggle now passed with little notice. Nevel's muscular legs were so accustomed to his riding that they effortlessly pushed the bike around gaping holes in the uneven road. It was freeing to be in control of his bike, riding alone down the long and winding broken roads that would eventually give way to red dirt paths towards the edge of the outback where he lived.

Nevel headed down Queens Street. For years, the lampposts along the street had featured the same faded posters beneath their flickering gas lamps, beseeching the citizens of Morgan Creek to step forward.

Our only hope is what we know. Are there bookkeepers among us? Reward!

The posters had been plastered over weeks ago by bold new signs that had appeared overnight. Only scraps of the scrawling prints were visible now, framed by sketches of battles and carnage. *WANTED– BOOKKEEPER*, the new posters seemed to shout.

Who among us threatens us all by withholding the information we may need to save ourselves in this broken world? Turn the traitor in and reap your reward!

2

Home

The same twinge of fear Nevel always felt when thinking of the posters crept up his spine. For years, Nevel had heard the rumors of battles breaking out across the globe over resources and expansion of powers, but like many, he wondered if these claims were false. It seemed so convenient, just another way the government could keep the citizens scared and in their place. No matter what he believed, though, bookkeepers were wanted and government leaders like Chief Commander Carrington would stop at nothing to have them under their control. Knowledge was currency, and bookkeepers were one in a million. Nevel swallowed hard after passing the lampposts and took a long hard look as he passed the barricaded library that was surrounded by local police while the bank sat vacant.

Storefront windows advertised the available trades from under green awnings. Nevel stopped in front of his favorite store with a three-tiered cake painted in white on the window followed by green paintings of cows and goats and chickens. Nevel rolled his eyes at the thought of someone offering up valuable information about the care of cows for a tiered wedding cake. Nevel figured someone would have to know something major, like how to cure mad cow disease, to earn a cake like that. Leaving his bike leaning in the shade of the awning, he entered the shop, which smelled of rising yeast and sugary treats.

"Well, if it isn't Nevel Walker! Come to satisfy that sweet tooth!" Mrs. Thomas teased from behind the glass counter as she wiped her white powdery hands on the tan apron that tied around her plump waist. Nevel smirked as he let his eyes fall on all of the cakes and donuts and muffins that sat tempting him from within the glass case. He knew he could have any one of them with the info in his brain, but he knew he had to make his purchases with only the amount of information a poor boy from the outskirts of town would have.

"What'll it be today, dear?" Mrs. Thomas asked.

"Just the donut please, Mrs. Thomas," Nevel responded while pointing to a plain cinnamon donut.

"You got a trade for knowin', lad?" Mrs. Thomas asked dutifully, although Nevel knew she trusted the fact that he always came with information.

"Yes, ma'am," Nevel replied and the two made their way to the curtained green booth at the exit, where the cashiers accepted the new currency in private. Nevel knew to offer just a bit within the curtained booth. He waited as Mrs. Thomas pulled out her logbook to take down the currency. Nevel always was nervous at this point, but he did as he had practiced so many times before, "I got a trade for knowin': Clover will balance your cows' diet and make the milk sweeter. It will also attract bees." It wasn't from his harvesting class, but Mrs. Thomas wouldn't know. Nevel watched her scribble in hieroglyphs—every family and business had their own note-taking codes to prevent theft—and then with her nod of approval, she closed the ledger and gave Nevel a smile. He watched, mouthwatering, as she pulled the donut from the glass case.

"Enjoy your treat," she said, handing Nevel the warm donut wrapped in a thin, papery rag that still smelled of the earth and plants it was made of. He hated the taste it left behind and, for a moment, he thought longingly of the paper towel rolls he remembered playing with as a child.

"Thanks," Nevel replied, quickly unwrapping the sticky pastry. He was out the door with his teeth already sinking into the first bite. By the time Nevel walked three feet to his bike, the donut was already disappearing in his mouth. Beneath the slight taste of dirt, it was sweet and sugary and soft. He easily could have eaten a dozen, but restraint was required to avoid blowing his cover. Nevel licked the remaining sugar from his fingers and folded the cloth to fit into his pocket. He could use it for a sweat rag later if needed.

Pedaling again down Queens Street, Nevel remembered being a young boy and riding in a car down this very street, strapped securely in a booster seat in the back, sitting in traffic alongside the trucks and cars as his mum sang merrily along to the radio. Funny how quickly things had changed. In eleven years, Morgan Creek, along with the rest of the world, had regressed back into the dark ages.

Nevel passed a white haired elderly couple sitting on a street bench surrounded by eager listeners, likely offering up wisdom of decades past. He swerved around a farmer checking his horse's hoof on the road outside a blacksmith shop, and whizzed past a quilter sewing on a stoop outside her shop. Further down Queens Street, a bunch of kids from school had formed a stick ball game in the street. Randy was at bat. Nevel swallowed hard and pedaled quickly by them, glad to have already finished the proof of his trade.

Just before turning off of Queens Street, Nevel could feel his heart quicken at the sight of Government Square. The square housed the jail, Chief Commander Carrington's Mansion, the courthouse, and the gallows. An Australian flag flew proud above another, darker banner. The New Commitment flag had been created with the changing times after the MegaCrash and appeared a few months after Carrington took control. With an iron book at the center surrounded by stars and a fist clenched at the top, the flag was meant to boast triumph over information but Nevel saw control over his mind and it sent goose bumps across his body.

Turning off the main road, Nevel cut through a

wealthy neighborhood. The houses were close together and loomed over the streets. They were several stories tall, with glass windows that were intact, unlike the broken glass pieced together outside of town. The homes were colorful in a world where colored paint was difficult to make and considered frivolous. Oversized, drooping curtains hung in windows, boasting the fact that every stitch of material they came by was not essential for practical use, but rather could be spared for ornamentation. Flowers grew in their front yards instead of food plots taking up every inch of usable soil. The families that lived in these homes were considered upper class, mostly doctors, shop owners, and political personalities like the Chief Commander's cabinet members. Many thought this neighborhood was still beautiful, reminding them of what had been, but the towering stories and decorative, useless lawns didn't impress Nevel. As he passed the grand home of one of Chief Commander Carrington's right-hand men, Nevel pulled his t-shirt up over his nose to avoid the awful smell coming from the stink lilies along their white picket fence. The government kept their dumping grounds out of town to avoid the foul odors, but the beauty of a stink lily apparently forgave its stench. It made no sense to Nevel.

Growing closer to home, Nevel passed the sheep and cattle ranches. These were fewer in number and further between than the mammoth, showy houses of town. With their corrugated metal roofs, the wide verandah homes were built for practicality. These homes often housed the whole extended family; grandparents, aunts and uncles, and cousins all lived and worked together on the ranches. These families were not as well to do as those of the government leaders, but they were respected as vital contributors to the community because of their meat, dairy, and wool. Nevel imagined being a rancher would be a decent life; he tried to picture owning his own ranch some-day, but the prospect felt as cold and empty as every other he'd imagined.

Nevel pedaled past it all until there was nothing but red road and blue sky. He always felt like he was leaving the world behind him as he approached the privacy of his home. Nevel's bike skidded when he turned at the pile of rocks that he and his father had stacked years ago to mark their drive. The terrain here was more difficult to traverse with loose gravel and debris, but it was Nevel's favorite part of the ride.

In the distance stood the Walker's home, miles past the rest, a lone sentinel on the border to the un-forgiving outback. This home was built by his father years ago in the only place he could afford. Graying weatherboard walls stretched skyward from the shady wraparound porch. The sun glinted off the iron roof, forcing Nevel to shield his eyes. It was a small, simple house, but to Nevel, it was home.

Nevel's black lab, Tank, had been waiting loyally on the porch for him as he always did. He lurched from his perch to greet him. In the bright sunlight, Tank's black coat shone, and it was easy to miss the telltale gray fur lining his mouth. A puppy when Nevel was a toddler, Tank had grown up alongside Nevel and was his best friend. Nevel was almost knocked off the bike as the dog jumped up, licking his face.

"Hey, boy," Nevel said, rubbing Tank's ears as he kicked the kickstand on his bike and turned to go in. It wasn't unusual for Nevel to return home to an empty house. In fact, Nevel rather enjoyed being alone. Although occasionally he would ride past a game of stickball and consider joining in, the worry would still be there that he would make a reference or offer a fact he shouldn't know. It was too risky to be in the mix. Nevel was safe at home. It was a relief to be home and not have to hide his abilities or feign mediocrity to deflect attention. An added bonus was the fact that, with his parents away, he was not being force-fed information. When Nevel was home alone, he was free.

Nevel headed to the couch in the living room, Tank still attached to his side. He pulled the cord on the dangling belt, which sent the ceiling fans spinning. It was an invention Nevel and his dad had proudly created together soon after the MegaCrash and had become the favorite aspect of the house. Using hub-caps from the old vehicles, blades they built from plywood, and thick rubber belts, they had created a system that sent the fans swirling with the pull of a cord, churning the still, hot outback air into a refreshing wind. When Nevel pulled the cord, the fan would start at such a quick spin he didn't have to pull the cord again for a good ten minutes. And for those ten minutes, Nevel could lay on the couch with eyes closed, perusing the books in his head.

Nevel scanned the shelves, looking for something to catch his interest. He enjoyed mysteries, even though he always knew the ending. The books he loved best, however, were about travel—guide, memoirs, photo documentaries—he read and reread them any chance he got, mostly when his parents were away and couldn't force him to save more of the literary greats. Nevel selected one of his favorites since childhood, a tourist's guide on the wildlife of China. The glossy pages had once been a prominent feature on his grandfather's bookshelf, but were now likely locked away in the city's library.

Nevel longed to leave Morgan Creek and see the world. Travel was still an option in the post-technological era, but it was expensive, dangerous, and complicated. The people who traveled were usually people who worked for the government and had trade business elsewhere. It would be hard to justify traveling across the ocean on a sailboat or for thousands of miles on a train just to see an animal. Animals fascinated him, and he loved to look at pictures of species in different parts of the world, animals he knew he might never see in person. There were still some zoos in operation, but the government had used many animals as barter with other countries, so the zoos that were left weren't exactly stocked with captivating creatures. Nevel knew he was lucky he could see things others couldn't. It was a blessing, a gift even, and he recognized it as such. He was bored to tears in school, learning repetitive lessons in home-making, gardening, woodworking, and more. He craved the chance to get home and read the books that were shelved in his mind.

Sinking further into the couch cushions, Nevel

could still feel the cool breeze against his closed eyelids as he flipped through the pages until he came to the chapter on the Giant Pandas. They were most prosperous when in solitude, the book said; Nevel could relate to that.

A pounding knock at the front door interrupted Nevel's reading and sent Tank tearing into the foyer, his booming bark echoing through the house. The hand that had hung over the couch to scratch Tank's ears now came up to Nevel's forehead as he thought about what this could mean.

It was unusual to hear a knock at his door. People simply didn't come to the Walker's home unannounced. U.B.M. members came, but always under the ruse of a quilting circle or some other preplanned event. Who would travel clear out of town to see him? No one good, that was for sure.

Nevel's greatest fear leapt into his heart. Had he been discovered? Were they coming for him? The thunderous pounding made him think of Blane Driscoll's Hulk-like hands, his stomach dropped like a lead block. Nevel made his way from the kitchen down the long hallway, running his finger absentmindedly along the bead board. He traced the bottoms of the frames bearing family pictures, his mum and dad's faces beaming in the dim light filtering through the curtains. But they were just pictures, and Nevel was here, alone, about to be taken into custody by the Devil of Queensland himself. Would he ever see home again?

Tank barked and ran circles around Nevel's legs, begging him to hurry to the door, but Nevel was careful. He reached the door, but paused before unlocking it. Looking through the peephole in the oak door, Nevel didn't see the police or government officials. He couldn't see anyone; all he could see was red.

3

Headache

The pounding of his heart filled Nevel's ears as he grasped the doorknob and turned. Tank lurched at the door, still barking. Nevel pushed him back with his leg and dropped one hand to pat his head and calm him.

"Can I help you?" Nevel squeaked out as he drew the door halfway open, exposing only the right side of his body. Through the crack, Tank now sprung forward and greeted Quinn on the porch.

Quinn stood smirking, fingers combing through her long red ponytail, which was knotted and frizzy from the wind. Tank's nose was poking at the shaft of her boots; she leaned down to pet him. Nevel was shocked that Tank licked her happily, his protective attack all but forgotten. Thanks a lot, Nevel thought.

Some watchdog.

Quinn didn't speak. She stood there in silence, her fingers running through the thick fur on Tank's head, her green eyes locked on Nevel. He shifted a bit in the awkward silence, waiting for her to say something, not knowing what to say himself. After a minute or so, Tank grew tired of the attention and trotted back inside, slumping down on the cool hardwood floor.

"Fancy a visitor?" Quinn asked, moving to follow the dog. Nevel stood fumbling, dumfounded, at a complete loss for words as she pushed the door open, forcing him to step backwards into his own home.

"I...uh...I..." Nevel stammered, then stopped. He couldn't come up with a thing to say. Quinn pushed past him, brushing against his hip, and she started down the hall, looking at the family photos as she went. Nevel looked outside for her bike as he closed the door, but saw nothing. How had she gotten here, he wondered. He had traveled home at a good speed. If she had travelled on foot, she would have had to run.

"Why are you here?" Nevel asked nervously as he followed her into the kitchen where she was opening cabinets and slamming drawers. Tank dropped a rag toy at her feet. She bent to pick it up, turning the slobbery knot over and over, before tossing it down the hallway. Tank chased after it, his nails scraping against the wood as he went. Quinn returned to her search, pulling open the cupboard to peer inside. "What do you want?" Nevel demanded, his voice still shaky. Quinn pulled down a tall, clear glass and tossed it to Nevel. He clambered to catch it before it shattered.

"I'll have a bit of water, thank you," Quinn said curtly as she turned out of the kitchen. From the doorway, he watched as she meandered into the living room where Nevel had been resting on the couch moments before. Tank followed, his tail wagging, the rag toy hanging from his open jaw. Nevel watched Quinn in disbelief. Who was this girl? His stomach twisted and he felt the sugary donut creeping back up his throat.

She pulled the cord on the fan and smiled as the blades spun into action once more. She moved to the table in front of the window and picked up a family photo before setting it down and opening the table drawer to look inside. She looked up over her shoulder and saw him watching. "The water, please," she said curtly. Nevel set the glass down hard on the counter and brushed his hair out of his face, crossing from the kitchen to the living room in three long strides and placing himself between the table and Quinn. He slammed the drawer shut and stared her straight in the face, daring her to challenge him. She looked dismissively beyond him out the window.

"Beautiful view," she complimented. She pushed around him and continued into the dining room, examining the shelves that lined the far wall. Nevel followed, glancing around for anything to hide.

"What do you want?" he asked again. "You can't just—"

"Oh," she said, and her voice was perkier than seemed natural. "I'm Quinn, by the way." She sounded almost sweet now, but the growing dread in

Nevel's stomach told him she was anything but.

"I know," Nevel replied, "from harvesting class."

"Right," Quinn said with a small nod. She was nearing the pantry when Nevel leapt over a dining chair to block her path. She couldn't open that door. If Quinn found the tunnels—if anyone found them— the U.B.M. would be compromised, trapped like rats in the tunnels they traveled through the underbelly of Australia. They stood in a dead stare in the doorway until Quinn spoke.

"You've seen the postings?" Quinn asked, her tone less flirtatious now, dangerous.

"Of course I've seen them. Everyone's seen the postings," Nevel said, his rage from the classroom earlier that day now returning.

"What do you think about 'em?" Quinn probed, suddenly looking him square in the face. Nevel felt like he was wearing a bull's eye in the center of his forehead.

"What's it to you?"

"Aw, just curious is all." Quinn turned from the doorway and headed back through the dining room towards the hall, flipping her hair from her shoulder as she went. Nevel followed, tossing his hands in the air in disbelief.

"Are you looking for something?" At Nevel's words, Quinn whipped around, backing him against the wall. In the dim light of the hall, her eyes gleamed, and he was reminded of the lionesses he had read about in Africa. Nevel gulped, but he didn't dare move.

"Yes, in fact, I am," she said, her breath warm

against his cheek. She leaned forward, her lips against his ear. "Show me your books, Nevel Walker."

You didn't just walk into houses and ask where the books were. People didn't have books; not anymore, and if they had books, they certainly didn't keep them out in the open on a shelf or even tucked in a drawer. Books were to be hidden, locked away, or tunneled beneath the ground in the hands of the Underground Book Movement.

"We don't have books!" Nevel said, but he'd never been a good liar and his poker face definitely wasn't fooling Quinn.

She glanced down and then backed away, her eyes wide, as though just now realizing how close they had been. Red faced, Quinn pushed Nevel aside with her right arm and began to brush past him down the hall. "I guess I'll have to find them myself, then."

This time Nevel grabbed her wrist with a tight grip as she tried to pass. "Don't," he warned, pleased to hear no pleading in his tone. "You won't find anything."

"Why not?" Quinn shook him loose and turned to face him again. "I know you have books." She paused, her gaze darting around the hall before locking with his. "But perhaps they're all stored in that brain of yours."

Quinn ducked beneath his arm and ran down the hall towards the bedroom. He leapt after her. Nevel wasn't the kind of boy to fight a girl, but this was too much. She fled into Nevel's room and leapt across the patchwork-quilted bed. Nevel brushed the hair out of his face and took a deep breath. Then he launched himself over the bed, but she was too quick and darted back out of the room as he hit the mattress with an "UMPH!"

Back in the hall she raced toward the dining room, knocking chairs over to evade him, but he crossed over them with ease and cornered her at the back of the room. Behind her on the wall was a framed black paper silhouette of a crow, the sign of the U.B.M. He had more to protect than just himself.

He was prepared to end this, girl or not. Nevel lurched forward, his forearm aimed for her throat, but she ducked again. This time, she knocked his feet from under him with her leg. He suddenly found himself on the hardwood floor with a knife at his throat.

"You are about to tell me everything you know," Quinn hissed in his ear as the blade pressed his Adam's apple. Nevel thrust his forehead at hers, knocking her off of him long enough for Nevel to sprint out the back door and into the outback, headache and all.

4

North

Nevel struggled to stay awake. He needed to keep moving, but his knees buckled beneath him and he fell to the ground. His tongue felt like sandpaper and his shins were coursing with sharp pains. His body was suffering without water. He had no idea how far he had run, but based on the sun's location on the horizon and the blisters throbbing and undoubtedly oozing in his boots, he thought, or at least hoped, he had put fifteen to twenty miles behind him since morning. Nevel desperately started pulling books from the shelves in his mind in an attempt to try to help himself, but they were all wrong; Chaucer came up instead of Field Guides to Navigation in the Outback, Shakespeare instead of Outback Survivalist.

The dusk painted the sky in beautiful oranges and

reds, and a slight but welcome breeze helped to cool him. Although it'd been years, he still missed the oddest things, like air conditioning. He remembered the long car rides to see Grannie and Pops, the cold, refreshing air causing goose bumps to break out on his arms, the scorching sun all but forgotten. He remembered nights spent tucked into his mum's side as game shows flickered on the television screen. He could still remember playing Wii with his dad, gripping the little plastic controller tight in his hand as he flew planes with the tilt of his wrist and paddled canoes by dipping the remote. It had all seemed so real with the sounds and the images coordinating in real time. That had all been years ago during the peak of the technology age. It was long gone now. There were no more beeping sounds and hand held devices. The TVs and radios were silent boxes. People wished now they hadn't digitized their books because they, too, were gone. The meteor changed everything.

Nevel jarred awake to the bitter cold of night in the outback. He shivered as he got to his feet. It was too dark to see even a foot in front of him; the only source of light was the blanket of stars spread across the expansive sky. Nevel pulled a constellation placement book from the library in his mind. Sleep had refreshed his mind a bit and, though more slowly, he was able to pull the appropriate books again from his mental library. Comparing the location of the constellations to the maps he had now pulled from Outback Geography, he could determine where he needed to move. He needed to head north, where he knew he would find rock formations that could provide a shel-tered hiding place. He was Quinn's prey and he had to put a few more miles between himself and Quinn before the sun rose. She knew too much and was hunting him down to find answers, but he wouldn't give up a lifetime of secrets to a girl in his high school harvesting class. He tightened his boots, and then set off in the direction of what he hoped was north.

Moving in the dark was difficult. Without his sight, his ears became more in tune to his surroundings. A chorus erupted from insects. Hooves stomped the ground in the distance like drums. The louder noises made him fear perhaps he was running right to Quinn, but then he would second guess himself and imagine a camel running toward him to knock him to the ground and he wasn't sure which would be worse. It was some of the quieter sounds, though, that really terrified him because he didn't know if they were his tired mind playing tricks on him. He imagined snakes slithering circles around his boots. He bumped into trees and saw shadows that darted about, making him consider stopping to hide until morning, but he was afraid of being a sitting duck.

When Nevel was little, he'd had a Superman nightlight in his bedroom. The night of the crash, it flickered once, feebly, and went out. Nevel sat up in bed and called for his mum. She came to his room and fumbled with a flashlight that wouldn't turn on.

"It's OK, sweetie, I'll be right back," she had said as he heard her fumble with another. The darkness was thick, deep, and rich; a kind he had never seen before. He even reached out with his hand to see if he could feel it, like a thick molten tar flowing through his bedroom. The digital alarm clock on his dresser was black. The green light that was usually just a spec on his ceiling from the smoke detector was gone. Finally, his mother lit a candle from the dining room and brought it to him. "Nevel, it is only dark to us because we are so used to our silly human devices. Imagine the animals in the forests and desserts. They love the dark." She wrapped her arms around him and drew him to the window. "And do you know what they use for nightlights? The stars!"

Nevel looked up to the night sky and felt comfort in the sight of Orion and Ursa Major. He continued to move through the dark with more confidence now. His mum was on his mind now; it was a welcome distraction. She had made the transition since the MegaCrash an adventure, keeping him excited about life. Together, they gardened and built things Nevel had only heard of in stories. But the best part—their little secret—was when they read books. While others had only one day a year to peruse the books of the library on Brary Day, they had the luxury of reading books as they passed through via the Underground Book Movement.

Bumping into a low boulder, he stumbled downward onto pebbly ground that felt different than the sand he had been on for so long. He coughed into his arm, trying to shield the sound. His throat and mouth were so dry he was having difficulty swallowing. Nevel let his hands explore the pebbly ground and he wondered if he had fallen into a dried creek bed. Immediately, he dug. He did not realize his fingertips were bleeding as he clawed at the rocky ground. The rocky sand began to feel cooler and finally the dry sand gave way to wet sand. A few more moments of digging and Nevel had a small puddle of water. Instinctively, he planted his face to the ground and began to lap the water up with his mouth like a dog. Nevel continued to dig and drink until his thirst was finally quenched. Wiping his sandy, wet mouth with his shirt, he stood up again. His fingers stung and he crouched back down to dip them in the little pool for a moment to soothe the cuts.

"You need to move north," he reminded himself. He hadn't even walked three steps into the breaking dawn when he heard Quinn yell. The sound carried from the south, or at least he thought it did, but he couldn't be sure how far away she was. Sound had a way of carrying loud and clear across this dry plain. "You can't run forever, Walker!" she taunted.

He swallowed hard and sprinted away through the brush.

Hours passed and Nevel was losing speed. Quinn was gaining on him, he was sure, and the thought made him sick. His thoughts kept drifting to the knife she had held at his throat and the lethal look in her eye. He fought to keep running, even though his legs burned. He couldn't breathe anymore; he could only gasp for air like a fish out of water. Normally full of the sounds of wild life, the outback seemed silent, the stillness broken only by the pounding of his feet, his wheezing breaths, and the angry growl of his stomach. He knew he couldn't keep going like this. He had to eat.

Nevel racked his brain for an easy source of food.

Flicking through ideas, he remembered a show he had seen on television years ago. It was about a man who tried to survive in different wild lands around the world. Nevel had been fascinated as he watched the man navigate through the wilderness, hunting prey when he could and eating bugs to keep from starving. That was it, thought Nevel. Bugs!

Grimacing at the thought, Nevel searched the ground around him as he continued to stumble along through the brush. Finally his eyes fell on a large rock. The man on the show had always found bugs under rocks. Nevel pushed the boulder as hard as he could. It didn't budge. He tried again, digging his heels into red sand. His lower back ached with the effort, but the rock remained firmly planted in the dirt.

In the distance, he could hear a scraping sound– this was no outback creature; it was Quinn scraping the rocks with the tip of her knife as she ran. The sound sent shivers up his spine despite the hot outback sun. She was getting closer. Nevel didn't have time to linger; he had to think quickly. He scanned his surroundings again and found what he needed. Nevel snapped a low hanging limb from a spindly Cooba tree a few feet away. Too late, he realized that the sound must have given Quinn an update on his location.

Nevel jammed the end of the stick beneath the rock. He took a deep breath, and then thrust his full weight on the end of the stick. He fell, his elbow now stinging from where the gravel scraped it, but he couldn't bring himself to care. The rock had lifted, slightly propped up by the stick, just enough so that

Nevel could reach under it. Dropping to his knees he grabbed the worms and crawlers before they could burrow themselves into the ground.

Nevel looked at a beetle and winced as he tossed it into his mouth. He tried to imagine it as a side of bacon to forgive the crunch, but the wiggling legs on his tongue made him gag. He chewed despite the welling up of saliva in his mouth that was predictive of vomiting. He forced it down and tried again, this time with a worm. It was meaty and tasted like dirt and the thrashing in his mouth was appalling.

He chewed and swallowed as fast as he could so he wouldn't get sick. He couldn't take the movement in his mouth; that was the worst part, and it turned his stomach. Nevel stomped on what was left and put the handful of crushed bugs in his mouth. He tried to imagine they were candy-coated chocolates, but he still had to gulp to get them down. The sound of Quinn's hoarse voice carrying across the plain reminded him again to move.

Tripping over pebbles and tumbleweeds as he ran, Nevel hoped the burst of energy from eating the bugs would kick in soon. The feeling of the wiggling legs on his tongue still lingered; he spit and wiped his mouth with the back of his hand. When he saw the insects' blood streaking his skin, he had to force himself not to throw up. "Never mind that," he told himself. "Run!"

"Happy Brary Day, Bookkeeper!" His mother's last words to him rang in his ears as he continued pounding his way through the brush, his boots throwing red dust up behind him. "Look to the moon, look to the sky, at the crow's call, it's time to fly!" Nevel smiled at the memory of her contagious laughter. The smile quickly faded, however, when he remembered that he hadn't seen his parents in weeks. "See you in a few days," his mum had promised. After Brary Day, it wasn't uncommon for them to be gone days at a time, but this time felt different.

Nevel was at a slow jog now as his mind spun webs. He was dog-tired and sick of running and hiding; he felt like he had done nothing but run and hide his whole life. He left school every day alone in a hurry to get home to the place he was safe. He was never on a team or in a club of any kind. He didn't have sleepovers or go camping with a group of guys. He had Tank and his parents, but sometimes it didn't seem like enough. For his entire life, Nevel watched other kids play like they were inside a glass box he couldn't crack open. He knew that was the way it had to be, but he couldn't help but wish he were normal. For the first time in sixteen years, Nevel considered that it might not be worth it anymore.

Up ahead, an image began to form, obscured by a cloud of red dust. Mirages were a part of desert life, but this seemed too real. Had he been running in circles? Squinting, he stopped and held up his hand over his eyes to block the glare of the sun as he struggled to make it out. By the time he could finally see the face, it was too late.

"Hey there, Bookkeeper, didn't think you could run from me forever did you?"

His heart sank. It was Quinn.

5

Captive

His feet settled in the dirt and he bent low, hands on his knees, gasping for breath. He wiped the sweat from his face and cursed the hot sun, the rocks in his boots, and his own failed navigation; his delirium had driven him straight to her. No point in running now. They stood not ten feet apart, the clouds of dust settling on their sweat-slicked skin as they struggled to catch their breaths. But even while tired and panting, Quinn had a certain calm about her that was unsettling, like a spider standing coolly over the prey that struggled in her web.

Nevel's eyes scanned east and west, but there was nothing besides desert and brush—no place to hide. He was looking for his chance to run, but who was he kidding? He was exhausted. He could barely see straight. He was caught.

Quinn drew a knife from her belt. She walked towards Nevel in three slow, long strides. "Don't even think about running again," she warned, twisting the blade between her fingers. The bright sun glinted off the polished steel; it cast shards of light into Nevel's eyes, forcing him to look down at his feet.

"I'm no good to you dead, Quinn, so what's to stop me from running again?"

"A whole lot of pain," Quinn sneered as she flicked the sharp edge of the knife with her thumb. She closed the space between them, the earth crunching beneath her boots. She held eye contact while she slowly pressed the flat body of the blade against the lump in his throat. Nevel fought to keep from swallowing. He narrowed his eyes. With one hand still holding the knife to his throat, Quinn shrugged off her backpack and rooted around in the bottom, producing a length of thin, nylon rope. She looped the end around his left wrist, catching Nevel off guard, and pulled it tight.

"What are you doing?" Nevel struggled, but the blade was still at his throat.

"Don't move," she growled, her voice low and menacing. She pulled it away, tucking it into the waistband of her pants. Before Nevel could react, she had wrapped the rope around his other hand and succeeded in securing his hands behind his back. She kicked his legs out from under him and he was brought to his bum on the dirt. He pulled at the bonds, but they only got tighter and his shoulders burned from the strain.

"What the hell are you doing?" Nevel's nostrils flared and his cheeks grew hot under his angry blush. "Didn't hurt you, did I?" She laughed as she pulled a canteen from her bag and took a sip, all the while walking circles around him as if sizing him up. Nevel took the moment to assess his situation. She was quick. She was smart. She was prepared. Nevel had on well-worn boots, not his track shoes, and he didn't relish the thought of running again with the blisters causing searing pain with every step. He had no pack like Quinn, full of supplies. She was obviously well rested, hydrated, perhaps even had a full belly. Nevel was running on empty. The only tool he could use as leverage was his gift, but he doubted there was a book out there that could save him now.

She drew an apple from her bag, tossed it in the air over Nevel's head, drew her knife, and sliced it in midair. One half landed in her left hand, the other fell at Nevel's feet. "Eat it, if you're hungry," she snapped.

"How the hell am I supposed to eat without my bloody hands?" Nevel barked back.

Quinn came at him with the knife. He flinched, eyes closed tight. He felt her on him and he opened his eyes in terror. Her fingers were quickly releasing the tight knots binding his wrists. Nevel rubbed his wrists, his hands tingling as the blood rushed back into them. He was reaching for the apple when he felt his legs jerked forward. Quinn was retying the knots that had bound his wrists, but this time they were harnessing his ankles.

Nevel brushed his hair back and rolled his eyes,

shifting this way and that in search of a comfortable seating position, but the ropes didn't allow much movement. After a few moments watching Quinn enjoy an apple a few steps away wearing a smirk, he finally picked up his apple and took a bite. Hunger took over. For a fleeting moment, he forgot all else as he tasted its sweet juice and reveled in its fresh crunch. Chunk after chunk, drool sliding down his chin, he devoured the fruit until he held only a few seeds and a sliver of the core in his palm. He wiped his chin with the back of his hand.

"So, who are you with then, government?" Nevel dug when he grew tired of the silence. Quinn started at the interruption, then smirked and perched a foot on a rock.

"Maybe," she teased. She pulled her hair loose from her ponytail. Her freed locks danced wildly in the breeze like flames reaching high off of logs in an intense bonfire. Her thin fingers nimbly combed through her tangles and then pulled the length into a tight knot at the back of her head. She seemed to be enjoying this moment of Nevel's clear defeat.

"Driscoll?" Nevel tried.

"Maybe" was all she offered. Now she opened her pack and seemed to be sorting, organizing, or maybe checking the availability of her supplies. Perhaps this was his time to make a move.

Nevel took a moment to really look at Quinn now. She was taller than he'd realized before. Her body was slender, but not thin—athletic. Her skin was fair and she had freckles along her arms and cheeks. With her hair pulled tight in a slick bun, her skin stretched across the sharp lines of her cheekbones. It only made her appear more severe. She wore a white cotton tank top and khaki shorts that appeared to be military grade with all the pockets and clips. Most of the people Nevel knew made their own clothes. The patterns were simple usually, with the occasional embellishment for special occasions. She could have afforded the fancy clothes, but these shorts were for utility and someone had put effort into them. It didn't make sense to Nevel why she would have shorts like that, unless of course her whole family was involved with Driscoll or the government. And this was certainly not what she looked like at school.

While she was distracted and his hands were free, he continued to talk, relying on his left hand to be very animated as a distraction while carefully reaching his right hand down to tug at the knots tied around his ankles. Without looking up from her pack, Quinn chastised, "Wouldn't even try if I were you. Those are trick knots; I invented them. There's no manual in your brain that will show you how to untie them."

Nevel pulled his knees up, wrapping his elbows around them, and hung his head in defeat. He swallowed the dry lump in his throat that welled up at the mention of the manuals in his brain. She knew too much.

She looked toward the landscape, perhaps plotting her next move, and he dropped both hands and began to try the knots again. The harder he tugged, the tighter they got until he could feel the sensation of pins and needles pricking at his feet. He gave up with a sigh. "The more you pull on them, the tighter they get. And if I am offended at all at your attempt to break away, I am not going to loosen them." She had turned back around and was pulling the backpack back onto her back now. "After a while, your feet will become so numb you will be begging for relief. Then your legs will turn purple because the circulation will essentially stop in that portion of your body. In fact, I have been trying to come up with a name for my knots and I think a great one has just come to me clear out here in the outback—the amputation knot!"

"Wow. You are nothing what I expected." Nevel didn't even realize he was saying it out loud. "Really? Should I take that as a compliment?" She walked to him now and sat on the ground opposite of him. "You just—" he started, careful with his words so the knife didn't reappear against his skin. "You aren't the same girl I sit behind in harvesting class."

"There's a lot people don't know about me. You ought to know the feeling well."

"What do you want with me?" Nevel asked, elbows still around his knees but now with his head up looking at Quinn who sat with that perfect posture that had blocked his view in class.

"You know bloody well what I want with you, Bookkeeper." Quinn leaned forward as she said this, her gaze narrowing.

Nevel's eyebrows furrowed.

"You're turning me into the government? You don't exactly seem to need the reward, Miss Uptown!" Quinn stood over him, her eyes blazing. "I'm not uptown!" she protested.

"I see your clothes, your metal-tipped boots. You

ain't exactly from my side of town!" Nevel looked her up and down from his place on the ground.

Quinn was pacing now; her cheeks flushed bright red as she sputtered. "Well, I have never exactly felt like I was Uptown, as you say, and recently I have figured out why. But it's not your business," she said, waving her hand as though swatting a fly. "You're right about one thing, though. I don't need a reward. But maybe I'm greedy." Quinn stopped and kicked at the dirt. She left her back to him and put her hands on her hips.

Nevel's mind spun uncontrolled to a history book shelved under government. Inside he saw flashes of pictures; emaciated prisoners reaching through the bars of jail cells with hollow eyes, hooded bodies dangling from gallows, bare-chested men being drawn and quartered. These were actual photos from history, but Nevel knew that now history repeated itself. Nevel's pulse quickened as he imagined his parents behind the bars of a jail cell. His pulse quickened again thinking of his own neck in a noose. Nevel shook his head left to right to clear his mind as he tried to reenter his present situation with more calm.

"Well you sure are too prissy to work for Driscoll."

"Not too prissy to catch you and tie you up like a cattle rancher," Quinn jabbed.

"Where are my parents?" Nevel demanded, tilting his chin up to catch Quinn's reaction. She was waiting, careful in her response.

"Your parents are missing?" Her ignorance about his parents seemed sincere, but it all could have been a ruse. She was pacing again.

Nevel shifted some from his seat in the dirt. He tipped both knees to the left and tried pushing himself to stand, but his feet were awkward tied at the ankle and he was forced to remain sitting. He blew air from his cheeks that tossed the hair off his forehead and leaned back on his arms, hands flat behind him with straight elbows propping him up.

"Well if you aren't going to tell me who you are taking me to, you can at least tell me the plan. Are we waiting for pickup? Are you going to carry me back through this outback to my sentencing? I won't go without a fight."

Quinn stopped her pacing in front of him and crouched down to look him in the face. "My plan, Nevel Walker, was to get to you. That, I have already done. What I am going to do with you next is still un-decided. For now, we stay."

Stay? In the outback? No one stayed in the out-back unless they had a death wish. Whoever sent her here would certainly expect an immediate return after catching her prize. So now Nevel had to wonder, was Quinn hiding something, too?

Quinn released the knots binding his ankles and then stood up, winding the rope back into a thick loop. She slung it over her shoulder and slipped her knife from her shorts, pressing it against his temple.

"Get up," she ordered. Nevel rolled his eyes, rubbed the sore spot on his ankles where the ropes had burned him, and slowly stood and stretched. Quinn grabbed his arm and quickly wrapped the rope around it. Nevel pulled back, jerked the rope, forcing him forward, and dragged her sharpened blade down his neck. Pulling his other arm in front of him, she wrapped his wrists together tight. His mouth was dry. He opened and closed his sunburned lips and attempted to lick them, but his tongue was made of sandpaper. His legs were sore from all the running, but he was glad to not be sitting with his feet tied so he could stretch his overworked muscles a bit.

"Walk!" Quinn ordered as she turned to stand behind him. Nevel felt the tip of the knife poke into his lower back, too light to draw blood, but he wouldn't put it past her at this moment to plunge the dagger in if he didn't move fast enough.

Nevel marched in complete silence at the tip of Quinn's drawn knife for what seemed like hours. The desert sun scorched his skin, drawing every ounce of energy from his body and leaving him pink and tender. He had stopped asking questions; she wasn't giving answers anyway.

Quinn was obviously not the prom queen she appeared to be at school. Nevel tried to imagine the rigorous training she must have undergone to become such a skilled survivalist. He pictured her amongst brawny military recruits, scaling wooden walls, crawling on elbows beneath wire in thick mud, and running miles with sand bags upon her shoulders. Or perhaps she was trained under men like Driscoll, forced to go days without food to prove her loyalty, her survival skills developed during late nights in the city, scoping for black market intel.

"Stop. Drink," Quinn finally commanded, thrusting a canteen at Nevel as he clumsily attempted to fumble with bound hands. He drank voraciously until the water droplets stopped falling into his mouth.

"You're shaking," Quinn noted with little concern. "You need to eat."

And with that Quinn drew another, much larger knife from her pack and tucked it under her belt. The blade was intricate and shiny, tapering into a smooth wooden handle. Nevel's mind spun to weaponry. "I'll need to hunt," Quinn said, dragging Nevel out of his stupor. "I'll need to tie you to something so I won't have to worry about losing you." He was surprised to find himself suddenly standing under the shade of an acacia tree. He couldn't remember moving, and berated himself for letting his guard down around her, even if only for a moment. "Come on, mate," Nevel pleaded, "I won't run, I'm too bloody tired."

Quinn rolled her eyes in disbelief. She pulled the knots from his wrists. "Hug the tree," she demanded.

"Hell no!" His hands free now, Nevel lunged for her knife, but she had her hand on it before he realized she had even moved. She pulled it from her belt to rappel his effort, and the blade sliced the tender skin between his thumb and index finger. A stinging pain shot up his arm. Warm rivulets of blood ran down his arm and dripped from his elbow to mix with the rust colored dust that stained his pants. Quinn shoved him against the tree trunk with the heel of her boot. Nevel hissed as the thorny bark scrapped his cheek. Ignoring the trickles of blood, she pressed his palms together and began to meticulously wrap the nylon rope around his wrists.

"You hunt, too?" Nevel asked, trying to buy him-

43

self time to figure out a way out of this situation. "I spend a lot of time out here. It relaxes me," Quinn said, shrugging, her focus entirely on the knots. "I can't believe your family allows—" He broke off when she tugged the knot tighter, pulling him sharply against the tree. A thorn nicked him just over his eyelid, and the sweat that trickled down his temple stung.

Quinn scoffed, and Nevel saw her shadow still for a moment. "They don't," she huffed and stepped back, admiring her handiwork. "What they don't know won't kill them. I'm sure you understand, Bookkeeper." She patted his shoulder condescendingly, and then her boots crunched away in the rock. "Hang tight," she called. "I'll be back soon." Nevel couldn't break free; the more he moved, the tighter the ropes became. The blood was still dripping from his wounded hand; if he was alone here for long, the dingoes would catch the scent and he'd be dinner for the wild dogs. His legs were free, but did him no good with all of the twisting branches confining him. Had that been Quinn's plan all along? There would be nothing to tie her to his death, even if the dogs left behind the bones.

Nevel scanned the pages of any book he could find about escapes—P.O.W.'s, Alcatraz, even the rock climber who sawed off his own arm—but nothing told him how to escape with no use of his hands. He then turned to an outback survivalist guide. There had to be something in there on how to ward off wild animal attacks.

As he waited in the heat, the aching deep in his abdomen told him he had to pee; now that Nevel thought about it, it was the first time he'd felt it since waking. That was a good sign; she was keeping him hydrated. Being tied to a low wattle, however, was hindering nature's call. Prisoner or not, Nevel refused to portray himself any weaker than he already had. He could only imagine what Quinn would say if she returned to find he had wet his pants. If the dingoes didn't finish him off, he'd die of embarrassment for sure. Nevel hoped he could shimmy his pants low enough to relieve himself and then use the twisty branches as leverage to help pick them back up.

Nevel sucked in his stomach, as far as he could, until his belly went almost completely concave. It was a trick he did as a child often, to get a laugh from anyone who would watch. It had been years since it was cool, though. He pulled at his core and as he held his position, his pants became looser and looser until finally they slipped past his hips. He sighed in relief until he felt the weight of his belt hit his ankles. They had fallen too far.

Nevel cursed his choice of going commando yesterday. Now, he stood half-naked in the outback, on display for the prying eyes of the wild. And Quinn. The thought of Quinn's return caused his entire body to blush red like the dusk painted across the evening sky. Nature was still calling and so he let go. Pressed against the tree, he had no way to aim, and some of the stream splashed back off the bark, spraying his bare thighs. He chose to ignore it; his eyes were on his pants and his cheeks were flushed. He remembered now that urine was used by campers to mark their territory and ward against predators. At least he was safe, although that did nothing to calm his nerves. If only he could shimmy his way down the trunk to reach his pants, maybe he could pull them back up before Quinn returned. But it was no use. The trunk widened as it got closer to the ground and by now, the amputation knots were so tight that he could no longer feel his fingers or the throbbing pain in his palm.

A sharp laugh from behind him caught Nevel by surprise, causing him to jump. "Lost your pants, did you?" Quinn called from nearby, and a hot blush spread up the back of his neck. He hadn't heard her coming.

"Don't look! Just let me loose so I can pull them up!" Nevel said, gritting his teeth.

Quinn dropped two headless rattlesnakes on the ground and stepped carefully around the puddle of urine at the base of the tree. Her nose wrinkled when she was forced to stand in the middle of it to reach his bonds, and Nevel noticed that her cheeks were flushed bright red, too. She tugged at the knots, but they only dug deeper into his already raw flesh. He hissed.

"You really did a number on these, Bookkeeper," Quinn said, her brow furrowed. "Another pull and you'd be handless, too." She pulled her knife from her vest and began slicing at the mess of knots; Nevel flinched when the blade nicked the sensitive skin beneath his thumb. "Hold still," Quinn demanded. "I don't want to waste any more of the rope than I have to." After a few more moments, the ropes went slack and Nevel pulled his hands free, quickly dropping to pull up his pants while Quinn inspected the frayed bits of rope, searching for pieces that could be re-used.

46

She pocketed a length about two feet long and tossed the rest to lie next to the snakes.

He sank down on the dirt, stretching his aching legs, and began to pick the thorns from his body. Some were large and protruding. He used his teeth to pull some, his fingernails to pull others. He twisted his arms and legs, searching his body for places that still stung. They weren't hard to find; the prickly thorns were everywhere.

"Getting them?" Quinn asked.

"Trying!" Nevel barked. He continued to scan his skin, plucking out thorns with his teeth and spitting them to the ground. Some left tiny holes that bled. Others just left his skin raw and sore. He would have to wait until he was alone to search out the ones in his more private regions, although they didn't hurt the way the tortured skin on his cheek and thighs had, so it might not be an issue. He realized now he was glad Quinn had returned so quickly instead of leaving him pressed against the bark deep into the night.

Nevel's body was in pain and he longed for the soothing effects of aloe. It grew wild in the desert, he knew, and he began to scan the area for an aloe plant nearby. It didn't take him long to spot one. He could see the long green pointy arms of the plant bushing out from a rocky area on the ground about twenty yards away.

"May I?" he asked his captor as he motioned toward the aloe.

"Go ahead," Quinn consented. "Just don't get any wild ideas."

He could feel her eyes on him as he leaned down

to pull an arm off of the plant. He knew now was hardly the time to run. He truly did need to make some repairs to his body before trying to take off again.

"Go on and pick a few, in case we need them later," Quinn called out to him. Nevel obliged reluctantly. Did she think she would be tying him up again later in the future? It didn't matter. He planned to be long gone before he would let that happen again.

Nevel walked back to where she was and tossed three of the leaves to Quinn, keeping one for himself. After splitting the thick skin, he began to pat the gel that oozed from the leaf into the red spots dotting his face and arms. It felt heavenly; the aloe was so cold on his skin after being in the heat for so long and Nevel realized his skin was sunburnt as well. Instead of just dabbing the red spots from his acacia injuries, Nevel began to rub the soothing aloe gel all over his arms and legs. It felt amazing. He rubbed it on his neck and face and the wind blew and a cooling sensation overwhelmed him. For a moment, he forgot all about where he was and he just reveled in the joy of the aloe.

A quiet moan caught his notice and he looked over to see that Quinn was doing the same thing— basking in the cool refreshing coating of aloe on skin. When Quinn noticed his eyes on her, she stopped and dropped what was left of the plant into her pack.

"We'll have to set up camp for the night," she said, wiping her hands on her shorts. "I don't want you running off, but as long as I have eyes on you, I won't keep you tied up either." Quinn paused and ran her eyes over him. She must have been taking stock of his weakened state and weighing the possibilities, Nevel decided. She leaned close, her nose inches from his own, causing Nevel to lean back uncomfortably to see her face properly, before she continued. "I think we both know that even with maps and what not in that brain of yours, you're no match for me out here. If you run, I'll catch you every time."

Nevel didn't say anything; instead he studied her as she set about preparing to cook the snakes. Like a scavenger, she quickly bundled dry twigs and small sticks. She kicked a few rocks around with her boots, making room for her fire. Reaching in her pack, she produced flint and steel and began striking for a spark.

Besides being a bookkeeper and memorizing every book flashed in front of him as his parents moved them through the underground, Nevel liked the way life had changed since the MegaCrash. Nevel had always been resourceful. He was glad to grow his own tomatoes, onions, and potatoes and snatch them from the garden to toss in a pot and cook for dinner.

He loved to hunt rabbit and squirrel and other local fare. He liked the feel of making his bike go by using his body's power. The technological era was held in such high esteem by so many, but he didn't miss it a bit; at least not what he could remember. Quinn seemed to be like him, resourceful despite the lack of technology.

As the small flickering grew into a blaze, she snapped a few thin limbs from the tree and pounded them into the ground with the heel of her boot, creating a spit. She skinned the snakes and tied them to the sticks to roast.

"Hungry?" she asked.

His mouth was opened as wide as his eyes and he finally lifted his eyebrows and asked, "Who in the bloody hell are you?"

"Well, Bookkeeper, that's what I was hoping you could tell me."

6

Questions

An immense orange moon kept watch over Nevel and Quinn. It seemed protective, maternal even, never letting them out of its sight. The outback was much quieter than it had been when Nevel had been on the run, soldiering on to find a place to hide. The night air was cool and Nevel was shivering, but he refused to admit it. The last thing he wanted was to look weak—well, weaker than he already was anyway—in front of the teenage girl who held him captive. The fire crackled and a wall of thick, still air separated Nevel and Quinn as they sat opposite from each other on the dusty ground.

The cawing of a crow broke the silence. He thought of his mother's rhyme again. When the words would leave her smiling lips, he knew she might be gone for a bit, but like the moon, she would always be near, even as she went to a place that was magical in his mind, a place from which she would return with treasures: books for his library. He pictured the framed silhouette of the black crow, which hung on their dining room wall, and silently prayed that she and his father was OK.

Nevel kicked his legs out straight in front of him and crossed his right ankle over his left. He leaned back on his straight arms, palms on dirt behind his back. His blond hair had curled a bit in the heat, and he brushed it out of his face with his hand. As they each sat quietly biting into snake meat, Nevel could feel his strength returning. He began to plot his escape. He couldn't outrun her, but he could outthink her. Nevel wondered if he should attempt to break her mental strength. He needed to turn the tables, to put the focus back on her Achilles' heel.

"Don't you know who you are, Quinn?" he called across the flames, happy to see her jump at the sudden interruption.

"I don't, Nevel," was all she offered in return.

It was the first time she had used his real name. Was she softening as he grew stronger and refocused? While there were still so many questions unanswered, the fact still remained that she had discovered him as a bookkeeper and was going to turn him in to someone. That simply couldn't happen. She was still the enemy.

"Sounds to me like we both need some answers," Nevel said.

"I thought bookkeepers had all the answers,"

Quinn said, wiping her mouth on the back of her hand and locking eyes with Nevel across the flickering orange flames.

"I memorize pictures and facts. I'm not a bloody fortune teller," Nevel said. "I need to know where you're taking me, who you work for, how you found out I am a bookkeeper!"

"Quid pro quo, Quinn,"

"Fair enough." Quinn took a long, hard look into the fire as if it were a crystal ball. She blinked slowly and seemed to chew on her thoughts before she released them from her mouth. "Just recently, the postings went up and they got me thinking." Nevel rolled his eyes. The postings had everyone thinking. "It must be lonely not letting anyone know who you are," Quinn's tone changed and her face softened. Her forehead was not wrinkled. Her eyes were doe-like now. "I am not that different. Everyone else thinks they know me from the outside. Do you know that I come out here, to the outback, every weekend by myself? I bet no one would believe me if I told them, but I feel more at home out here than I do in that fancy house in town."

Nevel slid to the right to bring himself just slightly closer to the side of the fire where Quinn sat. "Where does your family think you are?" he asked, annoyed with himself for being so curious. "Like I said, they don't care. Too busy. Too preoccupied. My dad is depressed; he goes to work and comes back and just goes through the motions." Quinn twisted a strand of hair around her finger, tying it in simple knot before letting it slip free. Nevel couldn't keep his eyes off of her. "Once I tell him I'm gone to bed, he never checks. I'll pop in every now and then through the weekend and he thinks I'm there I guess."

"That's a lot of travelling for you. You got a bike?"

Quinn shook her head no. "I like to run. It clears my mind, keeps me strong." Her gaze was still on the fire.

"But it can't be safe."

Quinn's gaze finally broke from the fire and she turned to Nevel with a laugh. "Seriously? I am a natural out here. I am safer here than in the misery of my loveless home." Quinn stopped her laugh quickly. After a moment, her face returned to a militant expression as she turned to look at Nevel.

"Anyway, since the postings I've had my feelers out and I noticed something different about you. You don't care about gaining information like the rest of the students. You're poor, Nevel," she said unabashedly. "You should be desperate, for your family's sake, to absorb every crumb of information offered, and you...you pretend to take notes and play dumb, but I can see it in your eyes. You don't have the hunger everyonc has to learn to survive—because you already know it all."

Nevel stared at her, trying to comprehend the implications of what she said. "You're telling me you figured this out on your own? You haven't been sent by someone? You're the only one who knows?" This was great news. This narrowed the playing field. If she was the only one who knew his secret—if she wasn't backed by a brood of adversaries—then she was the only danger. If he killed her, his problems would be over.

But something in Quinn's story bothered Nevel. It dawned on Nevel, then, how seldom he saw Quinn and how easily she had discovered his secret. If she had figured it out while still focused on Mrs. Downey's lectures on harvesting techniques, what was to stop someone else from finding out? Someone with bigger connections. Someone desperate for knowledge to sell.

"Don't get excited, Bookkeeper, I didn't say I was working alone. I just said I figured out you were a bookkeeper on my own." Quinn stood and grabbed the stick Nevel had used to poke at the fire and started poking at it herself, though the flames were plenty high. He sensed her urgency to cover her tracks. It was written all over her face; she had given away too much.

Quinn's demeanor hardened. She plucked up the large hunting knife and used her shirt clean it. Nevel tried to ignore the smooth skin of her stomach, which peaked up beneath the thin cotton. Red streaks of blood and dirt clung to the cloth when she tucked the knife away again. Her green eyes narrowed.

"I've given you your answers, Bookkeeper. You still owe me mine," she demanded coldly.

"Fine then, what do you want to know?" Nevel asked.

"I told you, I need to know who I am," Quinn said, still poking at the fire as he sat looking at her back. "I have recently learned I was adopted and I want to know who my real parents were." When Nevel didn't answer immediately, she prodded the fire sharply, forcing the wood to shift and pop. "Quid pro quo, Bookkeeper. Either tell me, or I tell on you."

Nevel rolled his eyes at the childish display. He stood and walked to where Quinn was. Grabbing the stick from her hand, he demanded her attention.

"Well, you're gonna have to start by telling me about you. I don't even know your last name. And what do your parents do, anyway? I mean, I know you are rich."

"Dudley, Quinn Dudley. And I'm not rich, the Dudley's are!" Quinn seemed annoyed by her own last name. She spat her last name out like she had spit out the skin from the snake they had just eaten—far enough away to break any association. "I'm not even related to them." She reached down to pull her knife from her belt. Nevel grabbed her arm to stop her and then dropped it as though burned.

"Okay, okay," Nevel said, holding his hand up in surrender, "I didn't mean to upset you; I just needed to know."

"I'm not upset," Quinn protested. "I'm ticked off and I would appreciate some answers. And you, Nevel Walker, are going to give them to me."

"Where would I be looking? Archives? What is it you need? Birth Certificate? I don't have a search engine option, you know. This may take a while. His head turned left to right as if he were scanning pages in a book.

"Adoption records for Alice Springs from 2022." Quinn said this as if she were completely numb. It made Nevel ache for her. He knew what alone felt like, but at least he had his family. They sat in the kind of silence that seemed to make the air heavy. Looking at her now, as the fire started to die and darkness veiled her, her green eyes and red hair were muted; she didn't look like a threat. She looked lost, and he couldn't imagine killing her, even if it meant saving himself. He felt sorry for her, but he felt something else, too, and it was unsettling. She was beautiful with her tough exterior stripped away, and she looked like what she needed more than anything in the world was a hug. For a moment, Nevel considered it, imagining his arms wrapping around her, her chin tucked in his chest in comfort, her ponytail flying behind them like a flag of surrender. No, he stopped himself. Focus, Nevel. She is the enemy. Nevel closed his eyes and watched flashes of pages covered in words and signatures. Flip, flip, flip, he searched the records in his brain.

"How does it work, anyway?" Quinn asked abruptly. Her tone was soft, but Nevel still jumped. "You have books just piled up in there?"

Nevel didn't answer right away. He looked at Quinn across the fire, trying to stamp out the things he'd felt. He focused on the streaks of blood on her shirt, the firelight glinting off of the small knife in her hands. She's still a killer, he reminded himself.

"Well, my parents trained me to shelve them like in a library because it used to all get very overwhelming. I got bad headaches after they fed me hours of books." He still remembered feeling as though there was too much built up inside of him, too many ideas and facts and images to keep straight. At the time, he'd wondered if it was a punishment for being different, but he knew better now. His parents were desperate to save the culture, and their son was their only hope. "Anyway, it works a lot faster when I am not being asked questions." Nevel smirked and Quinn took a step back from the fire, looking up at him with flames dancing wildly in her eyes.

"Right, fine, go on in that library in your head and find me some answers." Quinn sat, her elbows propped on her knees. Nevel sat by her, mimicking her position and closed his eyes.

It took time for Nevel to find anything. He had only memorized books he had seen. He didn't remember specifically if he had ever seen any book on adoptions or births, but his parents had, on occasion, brought through books full of data that had no meaning to him when he was very young. Nevel remembered his mother explaining that not all books held stories.

"Well?" Quinn was becoming impatient.

"I am trying, Quinn. I don't even know if I'll have it. I mean, my parents have fed me a lot of books in the last sixteen years, only some held local records; they said it was for leverage, I didn't know what they meant by it." Nevel stopped himself. He was giving too much away. She already knew he had seen a lot of books. He hadn't admitted to his parents' involvement with the Underground Book Movement and he hadn't admitted to having books of his own. He didn't know how much Quinn knew about the U.B.M., but he couldn't risk giving her cause to come after his family. Or worse, to tip off someone like Driscoll.

"Quid pro quo! If you want to live to see your

parents again, you'll give me my answers." Quinn had fire in her eyes. Her hand was clutching the knife handle, ready to strike.

"OK, OK!" Nevel said; he held his hands up in front of him to appease her. "I'm looking, I swear."

Nevel returned to the scanning: hospital registers, town censuses, archives, birthrights, archives, and adoptions. The files were endless.

Suddenly, Nevel stopped, stunned by the vision in his head. He looked again at the paper. It couldn't be right. He checked a third time, and a fourth, but the facts were there. His eyes popped open and he saw her in a new light. Of course she was tall. Of course she was skilled in survival.

"What is it?" She leaned forward. "You look like you've seen a ghost."

"There's no name listed," Nevel lied, even as the memory of the thick black letters sent shivers up his spine. "I'm sorry."

"You're lying!" Quinn jumped from her spot by the fire and held the knife to his neck.

The blade was hot from the fire and burned against his throat. He closed his eyes, but the signature still blazed in his mind.

Blane Driscoll. Driscoll was Quinn's biological father. He was dead where he stood.

7

Answers

"What did you see, Bookkeeper?" Quinn demanded, her voice almost shrill. Her grip on the knife was tight, her hand was shaking a bit, and her teeth were clinched.

Nevel stared at her with his jaw set and drew every ounce of courage from the pit of his stomach to protect himself and his family. He had to lie. If Quinn learned the truth, she may decide to turn him over to Driscoll, not that she wouldn't anyway. She was searching for her birth parents for a reason. She may be longing to reconnect with them, to win their favor. There would be no better way to win Driscoll's favor than by turning in a bookkeeper.

"There was nothing there, Quinn! The place where the name should be, it...it's blank. I just saw the name of your adopted father and it surprised me. That's all." Nevel told himself he wasn't completely lying. He had seen the name of Quinn's adopted father, Dr. Dudley. When Quinn had told him her last name, he had missed the connection. He hadn't realized her adopted dad was the town physician; he already had pegged her for the daughter of one of Chief Commander Carrington's staff.

"I saw your face, Bookkeeper! I bloody well know that you're lying! Spit out the name or I'll cut your throat!" She held the knife so close to his throat now that he was afraid to swallow for fear of getting cut.

"I'm not lying! Your dad, Dr. Dudley, he helped my granddad once. He is a good man. I am just surprised that you are. I mean, you are the enemy here and he is such a good man." Nevel thought his bluff was sounding a bit more believable now. It was true, too, the part about her dad helping his granddad years ago. "I was just surprised. That's all," he finished lamely.

Quinn dropped the knife from his throat and slumped to the ground. Nevel gasped for air and paced, rubbing his throat with his fingers.

"What's your plan now?" He asked. Quinn did not respond; she stared blankly at the ground, arms hugging her knees. "I guess you are done with me, then, so—"

"I'm not done with you, Bookkeeper," Quinn said, her tone biting. Her piercing green eyes were full of hurt and rage. "Maybe I will turn you in after all. You didn't give me what I wanted and now you are just completely useless. Unless I can get a reward out of it, become a hero of sorts. That might make my family show some love."

Fear bubbled in Nevel's throat again. No matter how he looked at it, she was still the enemy. Quinn was his captor, and he had to get away from her. He had to turn the tables. He couldn't outrun her or out arm her, but he could outsmart her. All he had to do was stay one step ahead.

Nevel knew that below the dry, dusty surface of the outback, there ran a vast series of tunnels, connecting all of Australia. They had been a vital component of opal mining before the MegaCrash. After the meteor hit, the use of the tunnels was vehemently restricted due to safety issues and mining halted completely. The government sealed the tunnels' entrances, and signs warned that trespassers would be punished, but the government was so spread thin that the tunnels were left unmonitored. Nevel knew they were being used by the U.B.M. to transport books. The old entrances were uncovered when possible, and new passages were dug. If Nevel could get to a tunnel, he could lose her. He could go home. He couldn't believe he hadn't thought of this before. If he had dropped in the tunnels earlier, maybe he wouldn't be in this situation right now at all.

He pulled *Opal Mining the Outback* and began searching for a map. Using landmarks, Nevel estimated that there was a tunnel entrance a mile and a half due east, marked by an assemblage of boulders. A dry riverbed lay nearby and would lead him right past the rock formation. He wondered if he could outrun her for that long. It would take more time than he could spare to disappear inside. For all he knew, it could be covered in rubble and he'd have to clear the entrance and dig his way through. He would also have to cover up the entrance behind him so she couldn't follow. It was a long shot, but he had to try.

Quinn, who still looked furious, appeared to be lost in thought. He knew this was his chance to run.

"I have to go to the bathroom," he told Quinn.

Quinn didn't respond. She didn't even look in his direction; she was hypnotically carving circles in the ground with her hunting knife.

"Seriously, Quinn, I've gotta go," Nevel repeated.

She turned to him, her green eyes hollow and cold. Her lips were pressed in a tight line, and her stare seemed to pierce his very soul.

"I will give you two minutes. If so much as a second more passes, I will come after you and I will not use my knife just to threaten you. We're past threats now." She stabbed the ground in the center of the circles she had been carving out of the dirt. Her demeanor, which had seemed hollow moments before, was now predatory again. "We both know I am faster than you. I will catch you if you run. Now that I know you don't have the info I wanted, I don't care one way or another about offing you." Quinn wiped the blade of her knife against her shorts and held it up towards the flames from the fire to admire its shine, "You get what I'm telling you, Bookkeeper? Don't make me kill you. Now go."

Nevel nodded and walked slowly away. They had been in an area without much cover, so he was glad to have to walk further through the dark to feign a search for privacy. He kicked at rocks as he walked and didn't look over his shoulder. He didn't want to seem nervous. At a large gum tree, he glanced over his shoulder and saw her still sitting where he had left her looking into the flames of their fire. He turned east and as soon as the tree offered its cover, he took off into a full sprint. He figured he had about a minute head start and hoped that the darkness would work to his advantage. Maybe it was stupid, but it was his only chance and he wasn't convinced she would really kill him.

He couldn't see where he was going, and for a moment, Nevel worried about what waited for him in the wild. He brushed the thought away. Quinn would have a hard time seeing him, and that was all that mattered right now. He had to get to the tunnel entrance. He was running faster than he had ever run, feet flashing forward. He could hear his breath flowing in and out and the dust trail he was certainly stirring up was surely giving him away. Still he ran.

He cut left and right, over rocks and around brush, trying to throw off his trail. He stumbled often and bumped into shadows that turned out to be trees. Soon the brush was clear and he assumed he was now running on the dry riverbed. He did not hear her call his name, but he was sure she'd noticed he'd run by now. She wouldn't be calling after him; she would be using her breath to run.

Nevel's feet rushed forward and his legs pumped harder and harder. Sweat dripped from his brow and red dust stung his eyes. His heels dug into every stride, launching him forward again and again. He was in a full-out sprint, unstoppable under the light of the orange moon. Nevel had a track coach once who preached about "the zone" when running, an almost trance-like state when the mind surpasses the body. He read about the idea of mind-over-matter plenty before, but this was the first time he had ever experienced the rush of adrenaline and the boiling feeling of invincibility.

Black silhouettes of landscape blurred in his profile. His legs were tight and he thought his muscles would tear through his skin. He struggled to keep his mind over matter. Focus, he told himself. Escape. Nevel continued to send his feet forward. He pulled his knees high with each stride, and pushed himself off the ground with the balls of his feet. He moved through the pain that came from the blisters between his toes and the sweat that stung his eyes. Nevel's legs propelled him across the dark desert floor. Suddenly, a pain hit him in the back of his head. Confused and stunned, Nevel wavered as the impact knocked him off balance and the momentum pitched him forward, skidding his face and hands on the dry riverbed. The back of his head throbbed, and a warm liquid dripped down his neck. Bright stars flashed in his vision, and then everything went black.

When he came to, Quinn was wrapping something around his head. He was still lying on the rocky floor of the riverbed. His hands and feet were bound. The glare of the morning sun overhead hurt his eyes as he tried to open them.

"I told you not to run, Bookkeeper," Quinn said, her voice almost teasing.

His head ached. His vision was blurry. She held a canteen of water up to his lips to drink and he realized that she was sitting with his head in her lap, nursing him back to life.

"What are you doing?" He asked, bewildered.

"Repairing the damage," Quinn said with a smile.

Nevel began to put the pieces together in his mind. Had she thrown a rock at him and knocked him unconscious? What he did know for sure was that he was now her prisoner again. He didn't know how long he had been out or how much time had passed since he had fled, but he knew the daylight meant he had been out for several hours now.

"I've been thinking, Bookkeeper," Quinn spoke so calmly. She seemed to be unfazed by the attempted escape, the cross-country race, and the recapture. Her hair was still in place, her body only slightly damp with sweat.

"Whatever you saw when you looked at my adoption record was interesting enough to cause you to risk your life," she continued as she smoothed out a wrinkle in the plant-pressed gauze. Her fingers brushed the wound, and a sharp wave of pain throbbed through Nevel's head. Spots formed in front of his eyes. "I mean, you are a terrible liar, but you might have gotten away with it. It's the running that did you in. Even knowing I would probably catch you, whatever you saw made you want to run. Whatever it was, it must have been huge to make you willing to risk every-thing. What would make you stupid enough to run from me again?"

"I told you, there was nothing—" Nevel tried, but Quinn cut him off.

"Ah, ah, ah," she warned. "Fool me once, shame on you. Fool me twice, shame on me."

Nevel tried to sit up, but his head was heavy, and he swayed uncontrollably and fell back in her lap. His vision was blurry. Half-formed thoughts swam in and out of focus, but he couldn't grasp a single one.

"You're starting to feel it, aren't you?" Quinn's face was now in triplicate looking at him. Nevel rubbed his eyes with his fists to try to stop the ground from wiggling. Shaking his head a bit, he looked to the sky, which was streaming with long lines of flo-rescent greens and purples and yellows. His stomach turned.

"What did you do to me?" Nevel's speech was slightly slurred and his tongue felt like cotton.

"I may have raided my father's pharmacy before our little trip into the outback. One to help you sleep, then one to wake you and make you talk," Quinn said with an evil grin, her green eyes narrowing. "What name did you see, Bookkeeper?" She brushed the curls off of his forehead with her knife.

"I... I didn't..." Nevel tried, but he could feel the drugs taking effect. His hands and cheeks and toes were prickling from the inside as if they were asleep. He could no longer feel the aches in his legs or his head. When he opened his mouth to speak, a bit of drool spilled over his lower lip and dripped onto his shirt. Embarrassed, Nevel tried to lift his hand to wipe it away, but his hand was lead, too heavy to lift.

"What was the name you saw on that adoption record, Bookkeeper?" she asked again, her voice sharper this time.

"Nothing." Nevel tried to hold out a little longer.

"I'm only going to ask you one more time. What was the name?" Quinn demanded, this time pulling at the golden curls on his forehead that she had playfully been tossing about with her knife earlier.

Like falling down a bottomless well, Nevel could feel himself trying to grasp onto anything to hold him back. He didn't want to tell her, he couldn't! But the drugs were making his tongue loose and releasing his reticence. Without hope, he barely recognized his own voice as it spoke the words.

"Blane Driscoll."

As everything faded to blackness, he swore he saw a tear fall down her cheek.

8

Dilemma

Nevel woke to boots by his face. Once pink, the boots were now dusky rose from desert sand, but they still reflected the sun with their metal tips.

"Get up," Quinn said, kicking at Nevel's ribs.

Nevel rolled over with a groan. His head ached still, but his mind was not as foggy as it had been. His feet were still tightly bound and the rope was making his ankles sore, but his hands were free. He had a terrible taste in his mouth; he tried to spit out the red dust that coated his dry tongue, but failed. He pushed himself up with his palms and waited for the nausea to return. It didn't. Wiping the back of his hand across his face, red-crusted dirt from both his hand and his face crumbled to the ground.

Quinn tossed him the canteen and he drank quietly, gulping down the slightly stale water, slowly beginning to feel like himself again. He didn't dare speak. Attempting to escape had been reason enough to strike him in the head with a sharp rock and drug him. Now, she had even more reason to be angry with him, and he didn't want to know the punishment that awaited him for knowing that Driscoll was her father.

The adoption record proclaimed that Quinn had been adopted by her parents from Driscoll in 2022. She was four at the time. It was clear that Quinn had been learning for the first time from Nevel that Driscoll was her father. The news was obviously upsetting.

The sun was low on the horizon. Quinn began to rummage around to get a fire going. Tumbleweed, a circle of rocks, and her flint and steel did the trick to get it started. Once it was lit, she sat heavily and kicked her feet out in front of her.

Nevel lay on his side and stacked small pebbles, only to watch them fall the higher the towers reached. There was no point plotting another escape. He simply had to bide his time. Quinn sharpened the blade of her knife against a rock, and the shrill scraping sound sent chills up Nevel's spine. Seemingly pleased with the fresh point on the knife, she started drinking from the canteen and seemed to be lost in thought. Nevel gave up on the pebble stacking and began skipping the pebbles across the desert floor. Suddenly, she whipped her smaller knife out of her pack. She grabbed hold of his boots and pulled them towards her with a sharp tug. The sudden movement caused Nevel to fall back, and he winced when his wounded head hit the hard dirt. Nevel couldn't see what exactly she was doing. A sudden pain alerted Nevel to the blade's proximity to his ankle, and for a moment, he imagined blood gushing from his leg, his severed foot lying on the ground. Quinn laughed.

Then, she dropped his feet and his legs fell to the ground, free of the constraints. She had cut the rope binding his feet.

"Gonna run now, are you? Go then. I'm done. I don't need you anymore. I got what I needed." Quinn's voice was rough, and her eyes were red, as if she had been crying earlier while he was passed out. She stood above him now as he lay on the ground, propping himself up on his elbows and looking at her through squinting eyes.

"Done with me? You chased me clear into the middle of the outback to ask me one question and now you're done with me? Why didn't you just pass me a bloody note at school?" Nevel was yelling now, the words clawing at his dry throat. He was inches from her face, and under any other circumstances, he would have been embarrassed at the spit that splattered her cheek, but he was too livid to even notice. Quinn didn't seem to either. Her face was stone. She held her ground.

This was ridiculous. He had actually contemplated killing this girl to escape her. He paced back and forth, scratching his head. She had threatened his life with a knife and this was the way it was going to end? He turned to Quinn, threw up his arms, and turned away from her again, continuing his pacing. Nevel looked at the ground. Her knife lay where she had

71

been sharpening it by the rock. He was sick of the threatening knife. He wasn't scared of her anymore. Nevel grabbed it and turned. Grabbing her by her long, red ponytail, Nevel pulled her to his chest and held her knife to her throat.

"Well, I'm not done with you, Quinn! I can't have someone out there, knowing about me being a book-keeper. How do I know you aren't going to out me? And what are you going to do, go team up with your real dad?"

"He's NOT my dad!" Quinn cried out.

"It's on the document, Quinn, clear as day." Nevel's hand was shaking, with the knife still at her neck. He didn't want to do this, but she had given him no choice.

"Kill me then! I don't care! No one does!" Quinn yelled, and then it hit Nevel—he cared.

Nevel dropped the knife and let go of her. She slumped to the ground and buried her face in her hands, swatting away the tears that were still falling. "I am just scraps that the Dudley's picked up! No one cares." Quinn's words were muffled from within the shield of her hands.

Nevel stood; his hand, which had just held a knife to her throat, was still shaking.

"I've had this dream for as long as I can remember," Quinn spoke through the awkward moment that followed their skirmish, her head now lifted from her hands, "of a koala bear mobile turning over my head, playing *Advance Australia Fair*. I had asked my parents if I ever had a mobile like that and they said no. But maybe I did! Maybe it wasn't a dream, but a memory!" Quinn sniffled. Nevel shuffled his feet in the dirt, feeling awkward and wondering if he should comfort her. "It doesn't matter, though. None of it matters. He's probably got a hundred kids out there. What would he care? He probably knows we're all sprinkled across the country and doesn't care a bit what became of us." She wiped her cheek with the back of her hand and took a few breaths to slow the sobs. "But it explains a lot: me never feeling like a Dudley, wanting to spend my time out here like an outlaw. It's in my blood, I guess."

Nevel wasn't sure if she was talking to him or just thinking out loud. Either way, he didn't respond. Unsure of how to react, he sank down to sit next to her and propped his elbows on his knees.

"What did it say about my real mother?" Quinn quietly asked, still sniffling.

"I got so thrown by seeing Driscoll's name, I forgot to look." Nevel sat more upright. "Hang on." Nevel closed his eyes and conjured up the certificate again in his head. He turned to her before responding, "Rose Driscoll."

Quinn's red eyes widened. "They were married," she gasped, her voice breathy and almost too faint to hear.

"Pretty crazy," Nevel agreed, "imagining Driscoll married to any woman." He didn't know how to act. He crossed his arms over his legs. He was glad her crying had subsided, but it still left them with awkward tension that made the air thick and impenetrable. The knife still lay on the ground between them where he had dropped it. Nevel wondered who would make the next move.

9

Exchange

The metal blade of the knife reflected moonlight. It made him uneasy; he stood and walked to the fire with his back to her. Something had changed within him. He was afraid, but this time it wasn't for his life. He was afraid for his heart.

He wanted to turn to her. He could hardly admit it to himself, but he wanted to wrap his arms around her. For the first time in his life, he met someone who he could relate to—even if she was the enemy.

"We're the same, you and me," Nevel whispered beneath his breath. "We can't tell anyone who we are." Nevel shuffled his feet and turned to see her reaction. She surprised him with a tight smile that tilted slightly up to the right. Quinn pressed her palms into the dirt, pushing herself up and brushing herself off as she walked toward the fire. Nevel put his hands in his pockets because he didn't know what else to do with them. "I don't want to chase you anymore," Quinn said, looking only at the fire. Her tone was quiet and calm, endearing even. Nevel swallowed the dry lump that had crept up his throat. It was quiet except for the crackling of the fire.

"I don't want to run from you anymore," Nevel said, his cheeks hot with embarrassment. He reached the stick far into the fire to push at an ember that could have been left alone, but it forced him to step once to the right so that their arms were almost touching. It was quiet for a few more seconds, and Nevel considered wrapping his arms around her, but his pounding heart stopped him.

"It isn't fair," Quinn said, seemingly dismayed. "What's that?" Nevel asked. "I don't think they should have taken our books.

We wouldn't be in this mess—me having to hunt you down for info." Quinn turned and looked at Nevel. He nodded, hands still in his pockets, and kicked at the pebbles on the ground. He was glad at the change in subject. Her breaths were still recovering from her crying, but Nevel could tell she was making an attempt to move on. After several minutes spent kicking rocks and staring at flames, she broke the silence again.

"Speaking of books, how did you get so many in that brain of yours? I mean, after the meteor, hardly anyone had books anyway because they were all digitized, but you obviously have seen a lot since then."

Nevel didn't know why he suddenly wanted to tell

her everything, but after guarding his secrets for a lifetime, it was instinct to continue to protect himself and his family. He brushed the hair from his forehead and said, "We had a few that my family had hidden when the government came to collect them. My parents made me memorize them."

Quinn turned and looked at him. Her eyes were still puffy from crying, but her gaze was direct, as her curiosity seemed to peak.

"But, you said they used to feed you so much. You used the word feed. I remember...you said you would get headaches and they trained you to organize them. You must have gotten in the library more than just once a year on Brary Day."

Nevel's cheeks flushed. He could feel her backing him into a corner, and searched for a lie that would appease her. Quinn's gaze stayed on him, her eyebrows furrowed in confusion.

"You were young when the currency changed and bookkeepers were called in to work for the government. You would have had to have access to tons of books over many years to build any kind of library in your head!"

Quinn was too smart for her own good, Nevel thought. It was dangerous for her to learn about treasonous acts. She was obviously oblivious to the Underground Book Movement, and he felt she should remain so. He had to protect his family, and now he wanted to protect her as well. Nevel pulled his hands out of his pockets and folded them across his chest.

"Look, Quinn, you don't want to know all of the answers you are looking for. They could get you in trouble. Let's just drop it, OK?" Nevel pleaded.

"Nevel, I just found out I am part outlaw. We're in the bloody outback where no one in the world is and no one cares who we are. Just let me in on the rest of it." Quinn's hands were on her hips. Nevel dug his hands back in his pockets.

"It's just not something you need to know," he said with a shrug.

"OK, what if I give you a little more? Something about me. Another secret," Quinn begged. She put her hands in her pockets and lifted her shoulders, her eyes doe-like as she gazed at him.

"I guess," Nevel finally gave in. She sure wasn't going to give up and he found himself desperately wanting to know everything about her.

"OK, you know how I told you I come to the outback alone a lot on the weekends?" She pulled her hands from her pockets and grabbed a rock from the ground and started tossing back and forth between her hands. "I like to hunt, but I can never bring the stuff back home because then my family and other people would know where I've been. So I've left a few rabbits and birds on doorsteps—you know, people who were down on their luck."

Nevel was surprised and warmed at the thought of her generosity.

"You're like bloody Robin Hood of the outback." Nevel laughed.

"Who is Robin Hood?" Quinn asked, and Nevel was reminded that she didn't know the characters in his head. He smiled, ignoring the sting as his cracked lips stretched into a wide grin.

"Never mind, that's nice." He said.

"Alright, your turn. Where do you get the books?" Quinn dropped the rock she had been tossing. "The U.B.M." Nevel said almost haughtily.

"The what?" Quinn turned to look at Nevel.

He stared at the fire. "The Underground Book Movement," Nevel said unabashedly.

"Never heard of it...you mean there are books out there that the government doesn't have?" Quinn's face was suddenly eager, her eyes wide as she took in this new information.

"Yep. Now you know why I tried to keep you in the dark? Now you could go to prison or be hanged for harboring a bookkeeper and for treason," he said, clapping his hands slowly, again and again, the sound carrying across the desert. "Congratulations."

"Wow!" Quinn leaned in, ignoring his sarcastic claps. "How does it work?"

"I don't know all that much. All I know is that there are plenty of books still out there and they are traded in secret," Nevel was proud that his parents were more than just your average boring parents.

"Unbelievable," Quinn said.

"So, out of all of the books in that head of yours, which one tops the list?" She asked.

"I've got a lot of books stored. I love the travel books. My parents always told me the most important books are the ones that aren't in my head—the ones I haven't memorized, the pieces of our culture that will be completely lost if I haven't recorded them. And then there are the books that aren't being written. I mean, no one is writing our history. They're all so worried about bringing back the past," he said coolly with a melancholy that seemed to send her into deep thought.

Quinn turned to him. Her thumbs were in her belt loops. Her head cocked to the right, she parted her lips and left them apart without saying a thing. Nevel couldn't stop his thoughts—the ones that made him want to grab her behind the neck and kiss her. He didn't understand where they were coming from. They had been enemies just moments ago; maybe they still were. He turned and walked into the darkness to catch his breath. She didn't follow or call after him, but he wasn't running away. *You don't fall for the enemy.* He paced a while before returning again to the fire, where he found Quinn setting up camp for the night. She had the canvas pitched as a tent, and Nevel eyed it warily.

"We should get some sleep," Quinn said as she crawled inside, looking at him over her shoulder and leaving space for him.

"You're right," Nevel said. He lay down by the fire, folding his arms beneath his head, and shut his eyes. He thought he could feel her eyes on him for a moment and wondered if she was about to say something, but then sleep took hold.

10

Siren

Nevel dreamt he was crouching under his desk at school in an emergency drill. His hands were over his ears to squelch the screaming crank siren that could be heard from miles away.

He was jarred awake by Quinn, who was shaking him furiously. A siren screeched in the distance. Jumping to their feet, they scrambled to pack up their supplies. Ashes lay where the fire had been the night before. Nevel shoved the canvas into Quinn's pack. In their hurried response to the alarm, their eyes met for the first time.

"Do you think it's an attack?" Quinn asked Nevel.

"I don't know," he said as he kicked sand over the ashes where their fire had been.

"What should we do?" Quinn was tucking a small

knife into her boot.

"We've got to get a view of town." Nevel slung the pack on his back and pointed at the large red rock looming in the distance. He scanned their area as she tied her hair up, and they both started off towards the rock in a slow jog.

Nevel was used to the sirens. Every now and then, the local government would notify the townspeople of an upcoming emergency drill. Families and schools and businesses followed protocol by hunkering down indoors and awaiting the official signals from Government Square. A repeat of the siren within five minutes meant all was well. Silence warned of a threat.

"It's probably just a drill," Quinn said between breaths, but the hairs on Nevel's arms were standing on end.

With every minute that passed as they ran in silence, Nevel's fears heightened. The new postings showed sketches of scenes comparable to the history books in Nevel's mind about civil wars, revolutions, and expansions of power. His parents were out there somewhere; his grandparents were in another town that could have already been hit. In his mind, he flashed to the letter his grandparents had sent him before the MegaCrash. He had not seen or spoken to them since then, but his parents had been able to get word via the U.B.M. that they were still alive, and they were able to send word to his grandparents that they had survived as well. Nevel knew his grandparents would never survive an attack like the ones he had read about in history where powerhouse empires came to take over areas as they expanded their power. No one knew for sure that these attacks were a viable threat now, but with the lack of communication and with swirling rumors, the government wanted to be prepared for anything. Nevel worried about his grandparents, even though they lived in another territory. A threat here could mean a threat elsewhere. This thought made him worry more than ever about his parents. He prayed this was just a drill.

As Quinn and Nevel ran towards the large red rock, they were in an all-out sprint, arms and legs pumping, chests high and heads back. Quinn kept a slight lead. Adrenaline coursed through Nevel's body and allowed him to keep up with the faster Quinn.

They were still about a mile and a half from the rock. The trees and shrubs were a blur as Nevel flew by them like a speeding bullet, his focus on the rock formation that would be their vantage point. His thighs were tight and burning, and his feet were throbbing. Quinn's red ponytail beckoned him from her course in front of him like a checkered flag signaling the last lap of a race. Faster and faster they ran towards the rock in a deafening silence, void of the signal that all was well.

At last, a long, screaming wail broke the silence and carried across the outback. It was the siren. Instinctively, Nevel and Quinn both immediately slowed to a halt. Crouched over, sweaty palms on aching thighs, they both hung their heads and gasped for air.

"That was a close one," Quinn said, panting. "Yep," Nevel agreed.

But their moment of relief was immediately interrupted by another threat.

"Look!" Quinn whispered, "Tracks!"

Not five feet from where they stood were tracks from a wind rover. Nevel didn't have a lot of information stored in his mind on wind rovers because they didn't exist until after the MegaCrash. What Nevel did know was that they were primarily made and utilized by Driscoll and his crew.

"Get down!" Nevel pulled Quinn down with him behind a gum tree as a wind rover flew by about thirty yards ahead. It looked just like Nevel had imagined them: a makeshift vehicle that was pieced together by the raw shell frame of a car from before they were rendered useless. There were no doors or windows, no fiberglass coverings—simply bars attached to wheels with a mast and sail reaching towards the sky. Nevel watched as a burly man cranked a lever behind him with his immense branded arm, while tugging at a rope in front of him that seemed to help his sail catch the wind. The man seemed to be scanning for something—maybe someone—as he cruised.

Nevel looked at Quinn, his heart thundering in his chest. She pressed her fingers to her lips and turned back to watch the rover. They were camouflaged beneath the low branch, where they lay flat on their bellies on the dusty ground. They were both still drenched in sweat from their run, and Nevel was still panting for breath.

"Reckon he's lookin' for us?" Nevel whispered as he licked his dry lips, tasting the dust that clung to them.

"We've been gone a while now, Nevel, in the

midst of a witch hunt for a bookkeeper," Quinn said between breaths, "I imagine it makes us look pretty guilty."

11

Hunt

From the place where Nevel and Quinn lay beneath the gum tree, waiting to be sure they were in the clear, Nevel found they were at a vantage point that showed the furtive lives of the ground animals and he was in awe of their strength and endurance. Nevel watched ants carry bits of plants twice their size. Worms wriggled and beetles marched across distances that were enormous relative to their proportions. Green lizards were twitching their tongues as they moved about and several quick rabbits scurried by, all cautious yet still moving on. Danger was everywhere, but these creatures continued the work they had to do to survive.

"The rover has been gone for a while, now. I think it's safe to do a bit of hunting before we scale the rock," Nevel said quietly.

"Scale the rock?" Quinn rolled on her side to face him. "I thought the second siren eliminated that from our plan?"

"Well, now we have to see who is out here looking for us and plan a way to escape. We need to get a bird's eye view to evaluate our situation." Nevel pushed himself up on to his knees and dusted the dirt from his shirt. "But before we climb, we might as well take advantage of the food that is running wild all around us." Nevel stood and pulled the pack off of his back, dropping it by Quinn, who was still on the ground. He opened it and pulled out a knife. He then swung the bag around his back and looped his arms through the straps.

Quinn stood and pulled out the knife she had tucked in her boot.

"Okay, meet at the base in a few?" Quinn said, and the challenge was clear in her smirk. She flicked her hair over her shoulder and turned sharply, setting a roundabout path to the rock. Nevel rolled his eyes and mirrored her retreat.

It was the first time they had been apart in quite some time. Nevel chased and stabbed at lizard after lizard, missing several and scoring a few to toss in his pack. All the while, he thought about Quinn. There were moments when he worried she wasn't actually going to meet him at the base, but he had the pack and she would need it. Then there were moments when he found himself missing her, wondering how her hunt was going, hoping she was safely making her way to the rock.

Nevel arrived at the rock, only to find Quinn leaning against it with one leg folded, knee up with her boot stamped firmly against the gargantuan formation. A good-sized rabbit was slung over her shoulder. The rock dwarfed her; she was an ant in its shadow. It stretched to the sky in what seemed to be miles. It was largely red, with a few small sporadic outcrops of vegetation, but it was complex with its ridges and juts and caverns.

"This should be a good spot for tonight," Quinn said as she pointed with her thumb to a small cave-like indention in the side of the behemoth rock's base. Together they walked to it, and Nevel immediately swung the pack off of his back and to the ground. He pulled out his lizards and laid them out on the rocky ground, one by one.

"Not bad," Quinn said with a wink.

"Well, it's no rabbit, but I don't have outlaw blood in me, so..." Nevel grinned. Quinn hit him on the arm with her fist.

Nevel pulled out the canvas and began rolling it in the red dusty soil, changing its color to match that of the rock.

"Camouflage?" Quinn asked.

"Yep, maybe we can hang it like a shower curtain to keep us less exposed during the last hours of daylight," Nevel said as he was already threading one of Quinn's ropes through holes he had poked in the canvas with a stick. Quinn joined him and soon they had a cover that almost spanned the mouth of the inset.

"What about the fire?" Nevel realized as soon as he lit it with Quinn's flint and steel that it might have been a horrible mistake. "Won't it give us away? The smoke will escape from our hideout."

"Maybe," Quinn agreed, "but we can't eat without it. We'll have to just hope they are on the other side of this rock. We'll put it out after we eat. It will be a cold night tonight without it."

They set up a spit and laced the rabbit and lizards onto a stick to begin roasting. As they sat across the fire from each other, waiting to eat, their eyes locked.

"What was the best trade you ever made?" Nevel asked Quinn, relaxing back against the rock wall.

"I suppose it was probably about two years ago," Quinn began, leaning back on her palms. "My dad had been really down and out and I wanted to cheer him up. My mum used to make the most delicious tomato pies you ever tasted." Quinn paused, and Nevel watched her blink herself back into the moment. "I needed some tomatoes. Our tomato plant wasn't growing a thing. I went to a neighbor who had the most beautiful red, plump tomatoes hanging from the tower of vines she had staked in her garden. I asked her if she might be willing to make a trade for her tomatoes.

"At first, she seemed annoyed. I was waiting for her to close the door in my face. But then, something changed. It was like a light bulb had gone off in her head, and she said that she might trade if I had one bit of information." Quinn smiled. "Then she asked me if I knew how to make wine. Of course I had watched my idiot brothers make it and I had the recipe down pat, from the grape crushing to the sealing and waiting. She took me into her kitchen, and I told her every

89

step of the process while she scribbled it on her paper, looking over her shoulder every now and then as if to keep a cheater from copying off her notes. I left with five tomatoes, and my dad loved the pie I fixed that night. It was the first time I saw him smile in months."

Taking a deep breath, Quinn continued, seemingly satisfied. "What was even better was that every time that woman got to drink her wine over the next months, she would drop some tomatoes at my door. It was the gift that kept on giving." Quinn grinned and wiped the dusty hands she had been leaning on against her shirt.

"That's great," Nevel nodded approvingly. "I didn't realize you have brothers."

"They are older and they are idiots. They don't do anything for themselves. They treat the help like dogs and they certainly have never helped at the house or cared about dad or me. All they care about is what they can get for themselves." Quinn paused and rolled her eyes. "Selfish idiots." She dug her heels into the dirt and rolled her eyes. "How about you?" she asked, steering the conversation away from the Dudley's.

"Aw, I was never very good at trading. I was always afraid I would give too much and give away my status," Nevel said and Quinn gave him a disappointed look.

"Alright, let me think," Nevel conceded. He thought for a moment before sharing. "Well, there was a time when a kid at school offered to trade me his bike if I could tell him how to keep the dingoes away from his farm and his pets."

"Well, what'd you tell him?" Quinn rubbed her eyes and yawned.

"I told him what the ranchers did to get rid of dingoes on sheep stations and what not—steel traps and baits and a fence. It was valuable information, worth more than the bike. But that bike has been my pride and joy," Nevel sighed, wondering if he would ever ride his bike again.

The meat sizzled, and Nevel hopped up and pulled the spit off the fire. He laid it on a rock between them. They began picking at the lizard and rabbit meat and eating as they talked.

"Quinn, I think we ought to consider the possibility that there could be some reason other than the witch hunt for a bookkeeper—some other reason Driscoll's crew would be after us. Is it possible that Driscoll is looking for you because he knows you are his daughter? Have you thought about that?"

"If he knew, why would he suddenly care now? It doesn't make sense." Quinn shook her head and tossed a piece of meat into her mouth.

"Well, besides us being missing and making ourselves look guilty by our absence, is there any other reason why they would be after us? And we ought to also think about the scenario if we were to be caught," Nevel said as he looked at Quinn, who was chewing hard in serious contemplation. "If they capture us, they will take us to him. They will take us to Driscoll." Quinn's mouth was flat as she chewed and she looked scared.

He understood her fear. Driscoll killed people for a living. He was a liar, a cheater, and a thief. The people of Morgan Creek feared him. The scum of the earth worked for him. Even the government bent to Driscoll's demands. Nevel had once seen a man tied up to a pair of Clydesdales and dragged straight past Government Square by Driscoll's crew. He didn't know what the man had done to upset Driscoll, but he couldn't believe the officers on guard would just watch him being pulled past, bleeding and screaming, and not say a word. Maybe even they were afraid of him. Driscoll was ruthless.

Just the thought of being caught by Driscoll killed Nevel's ravenous appetite, and he pushed his portion away. Quinn continued picking at small bites, watching him out of the corner of her eye. Nevel pulled out the knife he had hunted with earlier that day and began inspecting the dents on the blade. He was running his thumbnail down a particularly deep scratch in the metal when Quinn drew a sharp breath. He looked up to find her staring intently at the knife. He held it out and she took it tentatively, turning it over and over in her hands before clenching it in her fist, suddenly poised as though ready to throw.

"Nevel," she whispered with a gasp. Nevel ducked and then cautiously looked over his shoulder, afraid he would find one of Driscoll's men creeping up behind him. There was nothing but the dirt and the stars.

12

Poetry

"That's it!" Quinn jumped to her feet.

"What?" Nevel was leaning forward, looking around on the ground.

"Brary Day! It was after Brary Day!" she continued.

Nevel tried to follow, but he couldn't understand where this was coming from. "What was after Brary Day?"

"The competition." Quinn paced quickly as if she was trying to keep up with the words spilling from her mouth. "On Brary Day, there was a competition. It was just for fun. Did you see it? Like an obstacle course, but with running and sheep lassoing and...and...knife throwing." Quinn used her hands expressively as she told Nevel about the contest.

"There were all these boys doing it, one after another, for bragging rights. You know, their testosterone was pumping and it was drawing a big crowd. I walked by and some jerk whistled at me, like I was a piece of meat for him to throw on the barbie!" Quinn rolled her eyes. "And I lost my head a bit, I guess you could say."

Nevel shook his head. "What'd you do, Quinn?"

Quinn threw her hands up in the air and continued to pace and speak. "Well, I figured out that the guy who had whistled at me—who now I realize is probably one of Driscoll's crew—was the one who had scored the highest in the stupid obstacle course." Quinn stopped pacing and looked at Nevel with her hands on her hips. "I guess he was high on his horse about being the big winner. And so I challenged him. I asked if there was room for one more contestant."

"And then what?" Nevel asked, imagining Quinn on the course, outrunning every contender with ease. "I scored a perfect score. Blew him out of the water!" Quinn boasted, but Nevel's disapproving look squelched her brief celebration and she continued more humbly. "The crowd cheered and his face turned red and I turned and blew him a kiss and walked off while everyone laughed." Quinn stopped and sat, dumbfounded, as she seemed to realize how she had set her own fate.

"Geez, Quinn! That was dumb!" Nevel rebuked.

Driscoll's crew killed men for lesser acts. Maybe they were after her for revenge, but Nevel was doubtful. The hunt for a missing bookkeeper would trump any act of revenge.

94

Quinn buried her head in her hands. The smoke trapped by the tarp filled the cave, and they both were coughing. Nevel kicked sand over the fire to put it out and pulled down the canvas to let the smoke release into the starlit night. Night had fallen; darkness would be their cover now.

Suddenly, the sky became alive with wispy green and blue strings of light that danced along the night-scape. Effervescent neon chords moved to the wind's music; the images evolved and transformed against the black backdrop. Nevel gaped at the sight he could only compare with the pictures from the books in his mind. The colors were remarkable, the kind of natural hues that could not be categorized in a crayon box. Nevel snapped pictures in his mind and tucked them away for the future, but his eyes remained fixed on the phenomenon before him.

"What is that?" Quinn squinted and stood up, pointing at the coursing blue, purple, green, and yellow bands of light fluctuating in the sky.

"The aurora borealis. It was named after the Roman goddess of dawn, Aurora," Nevel spoke matter-of-factly, smiling wide. "They are also called the northern lights."

"Well, what the bloody hell are the northern lights doing clear in the middle of the Australian out-back? We talked about them in astronomy class, but they sure don't belong here!" Quinn asked.

"It's all a part of the MegaCrash. The magnets in the core of the earth are confused—that's why the technology stopped working—but it is also why a crazy mess like this happens. The northern lights have been tossed down here tonight. Who knows, maybe tomorrow night they'll be in Mexico."

"If there still is a Mexico."

They were quiet for a moment. Nevel knew there was no guarantee of what the rest of the world looked like since the MegaCrash, and it was a sobering thought. They sat down next to each other, eyes up at the sky.

"Read me something," Quinn urged when the last of the rabbit filled her stomach.

"Like what?" Nevel asked.

"Wow, I wouldn't even know where to start. Is it like you have your own library in your head? It's Brary Day every day for you, I guess," Quinn crossed her arms behind her head as she lay on her back, looking at the Northern Lights.

"Do you want a story? A poem?" Nevel was trying to narrow the search results in his head.

"A poem!" Quinn sat up and begged, "Yes, an old, old poem. One from long ago—back when things were like they are now."

Nevel had never heard Quinn this excited before. She was like a child at Christmas and he felt like Santa; it was an odd feeling for a sixteen-year-old boy. He was a bit embarrassed and shy about reciting a poem to a girl under the stars. Nevel wasn't one to seek the limelight; he rather enjoyed the privacy of the shadows.

"OK, OK." Nevel gave in to her pleading, "Give me a minute to look."

Nevel stood at the opening of their cave with the northern lights dancing behind him. Eyes closed, he entered the library in his mind. Strumming his finger alongside the spines of the poetry books, he stopped at a favorite. It was small, with a leather cover and thin, gold-edged pages. When he opened his mouth next, his voice was clear and strong. He spoke slowly, lingering on each word as if it were soaked in gold.

"Let me go where 'er I will
I hear a sky-born music still:
It sounds from all things old,
It sounds from all things young,
From all that's fair...
Peals out a cheerful song.

"It is not only in the rose,
It is not only in the bird,
Not only where the rainbow glows,
Nor in the song of woman heard,
But in the darkest, meanest things
There always, always something sings.

" 'Tis not in the high stars alone,
Nor in the cups of budding flowers,
Nor in the redbreast's mellow tone,
Nor in the bow that smiles in showers,
But in the mud and scum of things
There always, always something sings."

The outback was quiet. The Northern Lights danced. It seemed as if the stars and moon and every creature and plant had listened. Nervously, Nevel opened his eyes to see Quinn standing across from him with a tear sliding down her cheek.

"That was beautiful," she said softly. "Thank you." She spoke so sincerely that it was almost reverent, as though he had moved a mountain for her.

"It was no problem." Nevel sheepishly avoided her locked stare and stepped back into their cave. "We ought to go on and get some rest. Tomorrow we climb."

Quinn followed him silently back inside. Her footsteps behind him made Nevel nervous. He thought about the space she had left him in the tent the night before. He swallowed hard. In pitch-black silence, he sat on the rocky ground and she sat next to him, so close they were almost touching. He could feel her hot breath on his left cheek. He didn't dare turn to look at her, for fear of his nose bumping into hers. He lay down to avoid her, but she lay down too, turning on her side to face him.

"It will get cold tonight without a fire," Nevel said with his face staring straight up. He could feel her left leg slightly against his, and then her fingers brushed his arm. He pulled at the canvas she had used as a tent and put it over them like a blanket.

"Nevel," Quinn said softly.

He didn't speak. He couldn't. There was a lump in his throat, and his mouth was dry. Even though it was getting cold, he felt like he was beginning to sweat.

"Good night," she finally said. Nevel breathed in relief and closed his eyes.

Something was touching his hand—a spider, maybe, or a cockroach. Before he could swat it away, Nevel realized it was no spider at all. Quinn's hand grabbed Nevel's and pulled it towards her. She wove their fingers together and squeezed his hand tight. Nevel worried his palm was sweaty. He worried she would hear his heart beating outside his chest. But the squeeze began to loosen a bit, and her breath started to slow. Nevel smiled in the pitch black and settled in to sleep.

He dreamed that he was in Mrs. Downey's harvesting class, listening to her take roll. He could see his classroom from the vantage point of his desk.

"Duncan Berry." Mrs. Downey peered up from her glasses to look at Duncan's chubby face.

"Present," he said.

"Cindy Chambers." She cut her eyes left from her glasses to the blond in the second row.

"Present." Cindy mumbled.

"Quinn Dudley." Mrs. Downey picked up her hanky and dabbed her brow, but it didn't do much for the nervous sweat that was pouring down her face.

"Quinn Dudley," she called again, studying the empty seat in front of her. At the lack of response, Mrs. Downey scribbled down Quinn's name on the absentee list.

The names continued. "Lindsey Foster."

"Present."

"Betty Haynes."

"Present."

And it went on and on until she reached the last name on her roster,

"Nevel Walker." Again she grabbed the hanky. Again, it did little good to stop her nervous sweating. "Nevel Walker."

Nevel tried to call out, "present," but his voice was mute. He waved his arms at Mrs. Downey from his seat, but it was as if she could not see him at all, like he was a ghost or something. Finally after waiting a sufficient amount of time to allow Nevel to appear out of thin air, she scribbled his name on the absentee list under Quinn's name.

Nevel stood and walked to the front of the room, unnoticed by anyone in the class. He looked out at the sea of desks and saw that there was a thin man with slicked back grey hair sitting in his seat. The man was dressed in a suit, clearly government by his lapel pin. He traced the carving of a wallaby in the worn wood desk with his finger. At the very front of his row, an empty space gave him a clear view of the board.

Nevel woke in a sweat, but his hand was still holding hers, and it calmed him back to sleep.

13

The Rock

Nevel woke to find Quinn packing all of the supplies and the leftover scraps of rabbit in her bag. He stretched his arms long above his head as he lay on the red dusty ground. Then he looked down at his clothes disapprovingly.

"I think some of the wind and sweat has cleaned us up too much for our climb," Nevel said as he twisted to look himself over. "We need to blend in with the rock. I am going to roll myself around to make sure I'm the same color as this red dust that is all around us. You should probably join me." Squeezing his eyes closed tight and sealing his lips, he began to roll left. Like tumbleweed, Quinn dropped to the ground and rolled after him across the desert floor. Despite keeping his mouth closed, Nevel could taste dirt and he sneezed several times as the dust tickled his nose. He stopped and sat up, wiping his eyes before he opened them to look down at himself.

"You look good in red," Quinn said to Nevel, approvingly.

Nevel looked at Quinn. She was now coated head-to-toe in the red dust that would act as their camouflage and allow them scale the rock a little less conspicuously.

"You, too," Nevel said with a smirk, trying to ignore the butterflies dancing in his stomach.

"You sure there isn't a way to plan our escape from this place without having to scale this monster?" Quinn asked, looking up at the rock.

"If we stay down here today, they're sure to find us," Nevel argued. He looked cautiously out into the desert. "You may be able to outrun me, but you can't outrun a wind rover." The wind ripped through his hair; it was strong today—the gusts much stronger today than the light breezes he'd been accustomed to so far out here—and it reaffirmed his decision. He was scared, though, looking up at that rock and looking over his shoulder for the men who were after them. Fear was bubbling in his throat. He swallowed to keep it from pouring out of him. "If we get up this rock, it will buy us time, give us a place to hide while we map our route out of here." He studied the looming rock wall for a moment, searching for the best place to climb, before pulling out two knives from the pack. "We'll each have one in case our clothes get snagged or anything, we can cut ourselves free."

"Maybe they aren't after us, Nevel. Maybe they're

just cruisin' around," Quinn said pleadingly as she looked at Nevel. "We don't have to risk our lives—"

Nevel could no longer keep down the feelings that had been brewing all morning. They boiled over, and it was all he could do not to shake her. "Risk our lives? You've already opened that can of worms, Quinn! You are the reason we are in the bloody outback right now! We have been gone for days while everyone is looking for a bookkeeper to torture for information! They aren't after you because of your little stunt!" Nevel's blood was rushing. He stabbed at the side of the rock with a knife in his fist.

Quinn stood with her hands on her hips, narrowing her eyes. Nevel wanted to stop himself, but he couldn't. "Do you actually think they aren't out here looking for an evasive bookkeeper? Have you seen the libraries? They are guarded day and night by teams of police!" Nevel was leaning in to Quinn, and she was leaning back away from him. "Do you know why? Because they are like fortresses of gold!"

"I'm not stupid, Nevel. I know how valuable the libraries are!" Quinn kicked at the ground and walked away.

Nevel stormed toward her. "Do you?! Well, multiply that by a hundred! Maybe even a thousand! That's what I am worth to them! I am not as valuable as the books, I AM the books! They are a part of me I cannot delete or cut off or ignore! I AM CURRENCY!" he bellowed into her face. "I could be sold or tortured or hung for what I know. And now, because of you, they are on our trail. Maybe they still don't know which one of us is the bookkeeper, but they *will* if they catch us! It'll only take a few rounds of questioning under high stakes to reveal the truth. So don't complain to me about risking our lives!" Nevel turned and stomped off around the base of the rock, his face red from dirt and red from anger.

Seconds later, Nevel was sorry he had just berated Quinn, but he couldn't help it. Suddenly, he was truly realizing the situation. There was a good chance he would be caught. He stood for a moment and leaned his back against the rock wall, trying to calm down and catch his breath. A whizzing sound raised the hairs on the back of his neck. Carefully peering around a sharp curve in the rock, he saw two wind rovers searching the desert in the distance. Nevel turned sharply and ran to Quinn. He grabbed her arm and pushed her towards the rock's face. "It's time to climb," he said, his voice steady.

Nevel stood in front of the rock and rubbed his sweaty palms feverishly against his pants. He reached up, searching for a spot where he could get a firm grip, then heaved himself upward and planted his feet in shallow groves. The anger that coursed through his body from their conversation earlier fueled his climb. He passed Quinn and then had to slow himself to continually check on her below, offering her his arm to pull her further up the rock when she slowed. They didn't speak or make eye contact. Climbing was the only focus. Quinn was agile when the rock gave her the tools she needed, but she struggled when she had to pull the knife for leverage.

Finding crevices in the rock that fit hands and feet in the proper order was an arduous task. Nevel's boots, which had hindered his desert running, were proving their worth now in the climb as their thick treads offered good traction. He noticed Quinn's boots slipping several times. Nevel found his upper body strength to be a clear advantage as he lifted himself in many places where pushing with his feet wasn't enough to reach the next handhold. The further they ascended, the more often Nevel had to climb back down to assist Quinn, who seemed to be furious at the fact that she had no choice but to accept his help. He assumed she was still sour from his earlier words.

Finally, they reached a narrow ledge where they could stop a moment and catch their breath. It was only wide enough for them to stand side by side, their backs pressed against the face of the rock and their toes inches from the edge. Nevel's arms were slick with sweat, and his hands were scraped and scratched.

The silence was heavy, and Nevel finally spoke, breaking the ice that had grown between them since his outburst earlier. "I know the climb isn't easy." He looked at Quinn, who stared straight ahead, scowling, and he felt stupid for stating the obvious. He could feel the tension like a brick wall between them, and he figured he had to rectify it before they moved on.

"I'm sorry...I mean...I..." He stumbled over his words.

"You were right. About all of it," Quinn said. She turned and looked at him. Nevel couldn't figure out the expression on her face. "I'm the one who should be sorry," she said.

"Better get climbing," Nevel said to change the subject. They shuffled and twisted around to face the rock wall once more, careful not to get too close to the edge. Quinn dug her fingers in and began to climb, but the toe of her boot slipped when she pushed up and she wavered. Nevel grabbed her to steady her. Once he was sure she had her grip back, he let her go and prepared to follow her up. Lightening seemed to course through his veins when he touched her. It gave him the energy to push on.

A few hundred feet up, they stopped again on a ledge that cut inward enough that the rock itself actually provided them with some much-needed shade.

"This is a good spot to stop a while and rest," Nevel called over his shoulder to Quinn, who was struggling to pull herself up more than a few inches at a time. He crouched on the edge, and held out his hand to pull her up. "Come on, it's only a few more feet." The ledge was much wider, and they had room to sit and recuperate. As Quinn collapsed against the rock wall behind them, Nevel took a chance to look down and inspect the landscape below. "We are high enough up now that they shouldn't be able to see us sitting here," he said, confidently.

"How long do you think we've been climbing?" Quinn asked, her voice hoarse with exhaustion.

"Hours, probably," Nevel said with a shrug. He took a drink from the canteen, happy they had quenched their thirst this morning by digging in a dried riverbed instead of finishing what was in the canteen, and sat down to rest beside her.

"I don't think I'm strong enough to make it to the top." Quinn was gasping for breath; Nevel had never seen her so physically defeated.

"Come on, mate." Nevel poked her side playfully with his elbow. "You'd find the strength if Driscoll was behind you with a knife, wouldn't you? Just climb like your life depends on it!"

"Very funny," Quinn grumbled. She pulled the canteen from his hands and drank. The color in her face slowly flooded back as she rested her head back against the rock.

Nevel pointed up the rock and encouraged Quinn, "We're nearly halfway up, anyway, Quinn. We've got to get to the top of this rock to get our eyes on Driscoll's guys and to map our way out of here."

"You go, Nevel. I'll just wait for you here. You have a photographic memory; scramble on up to the top and take a few pics for me and then come on back down and give me the play-by-play." Quinn was smiling, trying to use her charm. Nevel began to realize that she was, in fact, serious. She had struggled up to this point, and if he had to keep retracing his steps back down to help her, he was risking exhausting himself to the point that he might not make it to the top himself. She was right.

"I don't know about leaving you here alone," Nevel said.

"You worried about me, Bookkeeper?" Quinn's spark was back in her eye now. It made Nevel nervous. "You?" Nevel scoffed. "I'm worried about how I'm going to scale the rest of this thing without your help!" They both were laughing before he even finished his sentence; the sad truth was if Nevel had to rely on Quinn to help him climb, he'd still be below on solid ground, and they knew it. "Seriously, though," Quinn, said refocusing. "We'll ration what we've got, and you can take the pack. I'll stay right here and enjoy a little siesta while you're gone." Quinn stretched and yawned. "You'll have to camp at the top. You can take the flint and steel. I couldn't light a fire on the side here or I'd be spotted, so I'll keep the canvas."

"Are you sure you'll be OK?" Nevel asked as they rationed what they had. He was worried about her being left without a fire to keep her warm.

"Yeah, I'll be fine! I'll keep a knife in case, but nothing's gonna get me up here on a ledge. I am as safe as can be," Quinn wrapped her rations in the canvas to keep the buzzards away. "You need to get climbing. We're wasting daylight; it will be too hard to climb in the dark." Quinn stood and held the pack out for Nevel to slip on.

"OK, we should have a signal of some kind, though...in case someone gets into trouble. Can you do a crow call?" Nevel looked intensely into her eyes.

The look seemed to catch Quinn off guard a bit, and she stuttered, "Uh...yes of course." She wrinkled her nose and let out a weak, "Caw!"

"That was terrible," Nevel laughed, and Quinn couldn't help but laugh, too. Nevel wondered if she knew how beautiful she looked when she was happy. Her mouth was open in a wide grin that drew up her cheeks and squinted her eyes.

"I guess you can do better," she said between laughs.

Nevel smirked and then channeled Peter Pan, puffing up his chest and beating it with his fists as he erupted with a loud "CAWCAW!" They both laughed. His adventurous cry had him soaring. He felt proud to be at the helm of adventure. The world was his. Before he lost his gumption, Nevel grabbed Quinn around the waist and planted a kiss square on her lips.

14

Fires

The lightening Nevel had felt earlier rushed through his veins. Quinn stiffened, and then her arms fell limp to her side. Her soft lips were still against Nevel's. Finally, her hands slid to the back of his neck, pulling him closer. She deepened the kiss as their bodies collided into each other. Nevel's arms hugged her tight, and their noses bumped a bit, but he didn't care. The kiss began to slow, and he pulled away and opened his eyes to see her soft face. He grinned, watching her eyes flutter open. Before she could say a word, Nevel backed away and hitched the backpack higher on his shoulders.

"I'm off!" Nevel heaved himself up the rock, his fingertips searching for groves to grasp hold of. He could still taste her mouth. He climbed quickly, adrenaline coursing through his blood. He wanted to shout another "CAWCAW", but he restrained himself. He had never kissed a girl before and he had never felt so alive. He wondered what she was thinking.

He imagined her still standing there on the ledge, dumbstruck. He didn't worry about whether or not she had liked the kiss because her body's response gave her away. The butterflies in his stomach lifted him further and further up the rock.

Thoughts of Quinn consumed Nevel, but his climb had to be his focus. He really had to concentrate at these heights; one false move and he could fall to his death. He created a mantra that he repeated over and over again in his head: Hand, foot, breathe. Hand, foot, breathe. It helped him focus. It kept him moving.

Nevel stopped on a ledge to rest and rehydrate when he figured he was still about a quarter of the way from the top. This particular section of the rock jutted far out over the base. He could not see Quinn below him and knew that he probably wouldn't be able to see her again until he returned tomorrow.

As he prepared to resume his climb, it occurred to Nevel that he needed to study the rock and mark points in his mind so that he could easily find her again tomorrow. He committed to memory the deeper ridges and odd-shaped juts. Ten minutes ago, he had passed a section that looked just like Tank's head—ears cocked with a wide smile; he missed his old friend. Just above this ledge was a section that looked like a low wattle tree, which made him laugh thinking about Quinn finding him tied to the acacia without any pants. Peering over the edge, he noticed that the path downward looked like the back of a croc; if he followed the line tomorrow, he should be fine.

With his body fueled, he continued his ascent. He did not dare look down. The dusk was spreading orange light across the plains, and the dimming glow reminded him he could not stop if he wanted to beat the fall of night. If he couldn't see the places where his hands and feet needed to go, he would be stuck on this rock overnight and he would surely never be able to hold on until morning. He continued climbing, summoning every bit of strength he could muster to continue to push his heavy body upward.

With one last launch of his hand above his head, he knew he had reached the top. Slowly, carefully, Nevel pulled his body onto the summit. Even at the top now, he still pulled his body like a marine in a crawl, at least twenty feet until he stopped and just lay on the hard ground, breathing deeply with relief. His body was shaky, sweaty, and sore.

The last of the sun was just about to disappear below the horizon. He had to get settled for the night so he would have the energy to descend tomorrow. He also had some reconnaissance to do. He stood to face the setting sun and knew immediately that he was facing west. Since the MegaCrash, compasses had become useless, and the sun was a vital tool for positioning. One had to be careful, though, to only use the sun at dawn and dusk when it was close to the horizon in order to determine position, for when the sun was high in the sky it could play tricks on you and cause you to lose your way.

The view from the top of the rock was breathtaking. Nevel watched the Australia he had only seen in books come to life. Kangaroos hopped, and koalas hung in trees. The outback stretched in vast desert and dunes in one direction, sandwiched between grassy wild lands and sandstone spires. He turned slowly, absorbing this picture of wild beauty. Brightly colored birds swooped through the darkening sky, searching for a place to nest for the night; the budgies, with their green and yellow feathers, and the pink and grey galahs splashed color against an otherwise red slate. Wild dingoes sniffed through a gorge near what appeared to be a desert lime tree with its weeping green branches. Nevel's mouth watered imagining the sharp citrus flavor of the wild lime. Along the grass lines, brumbies grazed, and Nevel thought he could see cattle and donkeys scattered amongst them; livestock that had wandered too far from their ranches and had now become a part of the outback.

In the distance, Nevel could just barely make out the wavy wind lines of the sand dunes. A few camels marched in a line along their ridge; the silhouettes of their humped bodies and the liquidity of their gate were hypnotic against the dusk sky.

In the shadows at the base of the rock, he saw an emu walking slowly. It was alone and frail. Nevel could empathize with the hungry creature. A dingo would surely take down a vulnerable creature such as that.

Australia, in all its wild, was beautiful, but also a bit terrifying. The deep outback was often referred to as the "Never Never", and he understood why from this vantage point. It seemed to go on and on, never ending. He wondered if he would ever return home. He wondered if he would ever survive this great adventure.

Snapping himself back to the reality at hand, Nevel got to work, registering on his mental maps exactly where he was. He identified the rock on which he stood with a map he had stored in his mind and could match dry river beds and other markers to pinpoint his exact location. He now knew which way was home and which way lead to other towns. Climbing to the top of this rock was worth it just to put himself on a map in his head. He blinked, taking mental photographs from every angle to store for later.

As Nevel turned in his scanning, what he saw next made him swallow hard. A sailed vehicle ripped through the desert. Another white sail glided into view, followed by a third. He caught sight of a fourth one in the distance. They were spread out, surely searching for tracks.

While Nevel wrapped the idea around his mind that there were more enemies than they had earlier surmised—more threats to contend with in their escape from the outback—he knew he had to set up camp for the night. So Nevel stopped his scanning of the beautiful and threatening view to gather sticks for a fire.

Nevel missed Quinn. He thought of the Emerson poem from the night before and how it had moved her. It made sense, the poem. Here they were, in a grim situation, but somehow his heart was fuller than it had ever been. Nevel smiled as he leaned back against the pack, watching the fire dance. The flames made him think of Quinn's hair, and he remembered, for a moment, the feeling the kiss had offered; it made him miss her terribly. His campsite was set far enough from the edge of the rock that no one from below would be able to see his fire. He felt safe and he hoped Quinn was OK. He assumed she, too, probably was safely tucked away on a ledge where no one could spot her from the prowling windrunners. He was glad that he could allow her some rest. He wondered what she was feeling since the kiss. Was she missing him now, too? The butterflies returned to his stomach at the thought of her, and he shook his head to regain focus.

He stood up to go take one last look out at the view before retiring for the night. It was dark and he was careful as he walked. Nearing the edge, he saw something that made his heart drop to his knees.

Campfires, at least thirty of them. They were everywhere; so many scattered fires on the ground, it was as if he was looking at a pond reflecting the stars in the night sky. The fires were spread on all sides, each separated by about fifty feet or so, and they formed a perfect circle around the base of the rock. This was more than four sailed vehicles; hundreds of Driscoll's men must be looking for them. If Nevel had any doubts before, the sight of their campfires washed them away. Driscoll knew exactly where Quinn and Nevel were. The rock was no longer a refuge; it was a trap. Now, all they had to do was wait for them to come down. There would be nowhere for Nevel and Quinn to run. They were surrounded.

15

Descent

Nevel tossed and turned all night. Rocks dug into his back no matter how he lay. What sleep he got was broken by the howling of the wind and his imagination. Several times Nevel sat straight up in a breathless panic, his heart pounding, certain he had heard Quinn's strained call. He reminded himself that she was safe, tucked away from view, and that while the men were encamped below, waiting for them to climb down, none had approached the rock themselves. Even so, he was eager for dawn to break so he could safely climb back down to her.

When the first hints of sunlight were barely showing on the horizon, Nevel was already preparing to climb down the rock. His mind was racing. What would they do? They would have no choice. They were to be captured. Even if they did evade capture here, they could never go home. It was too much to think about. He had to focus. He had to return to Quinn.

It was a slow journey, but eventually Nevel got to the croc ridge and rewarded himself with a drink. Though the descent was taking a lot of time, it was much easier on Nevel's body than the climb had been. He imagined the ground he could cover if he had had a carabiner and hundreds of feet of cord.

Nevel was glad for his father's love of the outdoors because it was proving to be useful to him on this wild adventure. His father was the one who had taught him about where to find water in the desert and how to climb and rappel off of rocks. They had done some rock climbing in the local park over the past two years, but with appropriate gear and at nowhere near the same heights as Nevel was today. If he were to tell the truth—not that he ever would—Nevel was terrified of just how high he was. He didn't dare look down, and he tried to distract himself with happier thoughts to keep his hands from sweating or shaking as he clung tight to the rock.

Nevel remembered a special moment he had shared with his dad on one of their climbs about a year before. Nevel's dad had been prepping Nevel for descent after a long climb to the top of a ledge.

"This always seems to be the easy part, son, but don't be fooled. Nothing worthwhile in life is ever easy. We can't just revel in the success of our climb and hastily let loose only to plunge to our certain deaths. We must take the time to fasten in, follow procedure, and focus our minds just as we had to in our climb. We have to think ahead and plan and weigh the dangers. You never celebrate at the top. The job isn't done when you think you've reached the peak. There's always more to do."

These were the kinds of words that made boys into men, and Nevel had known that as he accepted them.

"I understand, Dad," a younger Nevel had said.

"You have done well, son, keeping your secret all these years. You are smart. It is your gift and your curse. Don't ever let go and just ride the ride down. Be careful. Danger always lurks." Nevel remembered the cracks in his father's voice as he had continued.

"Your mum and I are so proud of you. You are an amazing kid. You know that right? Do you know how much we love you? Do we tell you enough?" Nevel had felt awkward at his father's brutal honesty, but he had understood this was a moment of sincerity he would remember for always.

"I know, Dad," Nevel had replied.

"Your mum and I are gone a lot. Like you, we've got our own secrets to keep, but we would never do it if we didn't believe in just how important it is. You, son, always are most important. Do you know that?" Nevel's father had been serious and intent on driving his point.

"Yes, Dad, I know. I've always known," Nevel had seemed to offer the words that his father had needed to hear.

"You know, I've always said that I don't care what you believe in, just that you believe in something. People have to have something greater than themselves to keep them humble, grounded."

"Dad, I believe in what you and mum do. It's heroic. Someday, I'll make you proud with the information I keep. I don't take it lightly. I get the big picture. Don't worry, Dad, I get it," and with that Nevel's father had looked at his son in a way Nevel had never been looked at before and then they had hugged and repelled. With every release of his feet, as he slid down the rock, Nevel felt closer to his father than he ever had.

Suddenly, Nevel's memories were interrupted by fear. His steady descent was broken in a split second. Nevel's left foot stepped to support his weight on a piece of rock, which broke off of the giant boulder and bounced and fell until it disappeared below. His right hand was not quick enough to grab hold. He was falling. He fumbled to regain control. He was sliding helplessly, the rock scraping his body as he attempted to hug it to hold on.

Nevel slipped powerlessly until he landed with a thud on the acai-shaped rock formation. Blood dripped down his shins and the palms of his hands. Shaking and breathless, Nevel pulled himself over to a ledge to the right. He was thankful to be alive and still on course, but he had been so close to falling to his death that he couldn't stop shaking. He closed his eyes for a moment and took several slow, long breaths. He reopened his eyes and used a small amount of water from his canteen to clean himself up. Taking a drink, his thoughts turned to Quinn. Although he could not see her yet, knowing he was close

119

made him feel stronger. He looked out into the brush and desert and plains. He didn't see the trackers. He hadn't seen them when he was climbing the rock yesterday either. Even at dusk from way up high, he had only spotted four windrunners. It was only in the pitch black of night that he saw all those fires surrounding the rock.

Was that a dummy threat? Had the men in those vehicles lit all those fires—giving the appearance that there were more of them—so that Nevel and Quinn would just give up and come out with their hands up? Nevel felt a twinge of hope spring forth. Four vehicles of enemies was a lot, but it was a lot less than a hundred men. Maybe there was a chance yet.

Nevel continued his descent, carefully lowering his bruised and battered body to the next ledge. He had been at it since dawn and he imagined it was at least four o'clock by now. He had to be getting closer. He worked hard to remain focused, fearing that the eyes of the enemy could be on him right now. He had so much to tell Quinn and he hoped that she was OK. They would be stuck on that ledge for a while as they formulated their plan. Originally, they figured they would simply drop to the ground and run home, but that was no longer a viable option.

Nevel was soon at the Tank rock, face-to-face with the wide grin. It made Nevel swallow a lump that was forming in his throat. Would he ever see Tank again? Would he ever see his parents again? He was hungry, tired, and scared, and the strain of the adventure was catching up with him. Nevel took a long, hard breath, holding back the tears, and regained composure. He was now just twenty feet from Quinn. He imagined a repeat of the kiss. The butterflies were back.

Lowering himself down the final portions of the rock's face, Nevel landed on Quinn's ledge with a huge smile on his face; but his smile shattered into a million pieces because there were no arms to greet him, no freckled smiles at their reunion. Quinn was gone.

16

Crow

Where was she? Nevel walked about the small ledge in disbelief. He scratched his head and bit his lip. Her canvas was on the ground, but there was no other sign of her. Had she been taken? Did she leave him? She couldn't have; there was nowhere to go.

Nevel looked over the edge for any signs from below. He didn't see her broken body down below. He didn't see tracks on the ground. He didn't hear voices or the hum of wheels carried by sails. He looked back at the ledge as a pit grew in his belly.

Picking up the canvas, he shook it to see if there was more evidence of any kind. He scoured the rock floor to look for signs of struggle or even blood, but he found nothing.

Nevel looked up at the rock wall he'd just descended. Had she climbed? Did she have to get away? He had just come down that way. Had he paid attention to details during his descent? He couldn't imagine she had gone up. He would have seen her. Her knife wasn't here. This was a key piece of evidence. If there had been a struggle in which she lost, surely the knife would have fallen to the ground. There was only one thing he knew for sure; Quinn was gone.

Nevel wiped his sweaty eyes and slumped onto the ground in disbelief. Frustrated, he picked up a piece of rock and tossed it over his head.

"Ow!" Quinn cried from behind him.

Nevel spun around to see Quinn rubbing her head where the rock had hit her. He jumped up and threw his arms around her, picking her up and spinning her off of her feet.

"Where did you come from? I...I thought you were gone." Nevel couldn't believe it. It was as if she appeared out of vapor.

"I am so sorry, Nevel, I didn't mean to scare you," Quinn apologized as she wrapped arms and legs around him in a tight bear hug. When she pulled her face back to look at Nevel, he shied away and set her down.

"There was a crevice at the back of this ledge; it was covered in vines, so we didn't notice it; but it leads into a rock hallway of sorts, and there's some vegetation back there that I was gathering." Quinn pointed at the vines. She grabbed his hand and led him towards them. "I'm so glad you are back! Are you OK?" Quinn was seemingly fine—perfect even. Nevel was speechless. When he didn't respond, Quinn grabbed hold of his hand and pulled him away from the edge. "Come on, I'll show you!" She laughed. He squeezed her hand tight and followed her back behind a curtain of vines, in between the rocks at the back of the ledge.

After squeezing through a narrow passage in the rocks—they had to move through sideways with their breaths held in to avoid getting stuck—they came to an opening. It was like walking into a secret garden. The walls of the open cave were damp and covered in vines, and sprigs of green were everywhere. The cavern was round, and the ceiling opened to a hole that was about four feet across, so there was cool shade as well as sunshine. Nevel's eyes were wide. He couldn't believe this place existed halfway up the rock.

"I didn't find it until this morning," Quinn explained. "I was looking for bugs on the vines and then realized that there was no rock behind them. I just couldn't believe it when I saw this place! Isn't it amazing?" Quinn walked around, pointing and gesturing with her hands as if she were showing off a new apartment. Nevel followed, taking it all in.

"Who would have thought we would find a secret rock garden in the middle of the desert?" Quinn asked, but Nevel was at a loss for words. He ran his hands across the walls and gazed in awe at the hole in the top.

"Well, anyway, I didn't mean to scare you by not being on the ledge when you got back." Quinn was facing Nevel with her hands on her hips. "I've been checking every few minutes to see if I could see you." Nevel was still running his hands along the rocks and absorbing this place in awe as Quinn continued. "Now, tell me about your night. How was the climb? Are you so tired? What did you see?"

Nevel laughed at her chattering. "Well, you certainly got plenty of rest."

"I haven't spoken since you left, Bookkeeper. I imagine I have been holding it all in. And, yes, thanks to you, I slept like a baby! OK, your turn to turn on the chatter."

"It's not exactly good news, Quinn," Nevel warned. He proceeded to tell her all about the four vehicles, the fires encircling the rock, and the possibility that there might be just the wind rovers standing between them and their freedom. Nevel looked at Quinn for reassurance, but it wasn't what she was giving.

"Freedom? What freedom, Nevel? We are trapped, and even if we get off of this rock, we can't go home." Quinn's green eyes dimmed, and they sat trying to think of a plan. The mood had flipped like a switch from excitement to dread.

"This secret cave is buying us time," Nevel blurted out, desperate to hold onto the hopeful feeling he'd had before. "We can stay here tonight and figure it out. By tomorrow, even the grass and bugs won't sustain us. We'll have to move out."

"OK," said Quinn, but she still looked worried.

"I'm going to get the stuff off the ledge and bring it in here, so if we are being watched, they'll think we have moved on from this spot. I don't think they'll climb after us. They have the advantage being on the ground and they know it will only be a matter of time before we have to come down." Nevel wasn't giving up. He strode to the front of the ledge, grabbed the pack and the canvas, and scoured the ground for anything else that might have been left behind. He was careful not to pull at the vines as he slipped through the narrow passage, intent on keeping their cover. They were going to survive this.

Things just weren't going as planned, but Nevel was grateful for the hideaway. His skin was fried from being in the blaring sun scaling the rock for two days. He took his shirt off and lay down on the cool, wet stone floor. He swore he could hear his skin sizzle as it met the rock and he let out a long yawn.

Quinn looked at Nevel and then walked about the space, busying herself by picking at the vegetation. "You rest, Nevel, I'm not tired just yet," Quinn said. Nevel fell into a restless sleep and dreamed of black birds and fireballs and throwing knives. Quinn sat by his side, putting cool wet leaves on his forehead and wiping the sweat from his cheek with his t-shirt.

Morning came as a surprise. Nevel hadn't meant to sleep from the afternoon on through until the dawn.

"I'm sorry," Nevel apologized as he opened his eyes to daylight and found Quinn watching him.

"No worries, you needed your sleep. You didn't miss a thing," Quinn said.

"Did you sleep?" Nevel asked, sitting up. His body still ached from the strenuous rock climbing.

"Oh, here and there," Quinn replied, but she

looked refreshed. "I have a surprise for you!"

"A surprise?" Nevel was still waking and was confused by her positive outlook.

"I was bored; you slept a lot. There still was a lot of daylight, so I explored a bit and I found the coolest thing. I think you'll like it. Come over here, and I'll show you."

Nevel wiped the sleep out of his eyes before grabbing his t-shirt and pulling it on. He followed Quinn a few feet to the other side of their little cave and watched her as she pulled back some vines to expose the rock wall behind them. Nevel squinted, but he couldn't see a thing. "You have to look closer. Do you see a picture?"

Quinn asked. As she traced it with her finger, Nevel did see a faint picture that had been carved into the rock.

"A crow!" Nevel threw up his hands and shouted, surprising Quinn and almost sending her to the ground with his flailing arms. He couldn't believe it.

There was hope.

"What in the world, Nevel? I just thought it was cool; it was weird that we had decided our secret call would be the call of the crow, and then here I find this secret cave with a picture of a crow in it! Ha! What are the chances?" Quinn was laughing, but Nevel's eyes were wide, scanning the rest of the cave frantically with his mouth wide open in shock.

"Quinn, do you know what this means?" Nevel asked, turning to face her.

"Not a clue," Quinn responded, with raised eyebrows.

"The crow," Nevel told her with intensity, "is a sign of the U.B.M. They use it to mark spots where they drop off books and where they rendezvous for pick-up. Sometimes they even use the crow to mark their tunnels. There could be more to this cave, Quinn. Start looking!"

Nevel was an expert on the U.B.M., and it made sense. They both began to search the stone walls, brushing away vines, testing for loose spots in the rock. Nevel was sliding his hands up and down the cool, wet walls, feeling for cracks or markings. When they found nothing, they returned to the crow to examine it more closely.

"Does it look like it is pointing in a certain direction to you?" Nevel asked.

"The beak seems to point to the right and a little bit down," Quinn said, gesturing towards the ground. Nevel crouched low near the spot where she had indicated and waddled to the right as he ran his fingers along the line where the wall met the floor. He moved slowly, feeling the tightness in his thighs from his crouch, and then he dropped to his hands and knees in a searching crawl. Quinn joined him. The rock floor was hard, and they were putting such pressure on their kneecaps as they searched that Nevel's began to bleed. Suddenly Nevel stopped and looked at Quinn with a wide grin.

"Quinn." He had a look of sheer joy on his face, "I think I found a door."

17

Depository

Quinn and Nevel pushed with every bit of their strength against a piece of rock no bigger than four feet tall. It took a few tries, but eventually it pushed open. Cool, moist air escaped from the space and brushed against Nevel's cheeks. All they could see was darkness.

"We need a light," Nevel said and he tore open the pack, grabbing the flint and steel. Nevel looked around for something to make as a torch. He chose a pile of reeds and struck the flint.

"After you," Quinn said, flattening herself against the wall to let Nevel pass and lead the way. Nevel wondered if Quinn could hear his heart beating through his chest. The ground was hard and gritty and it hurt his knees as he dragged them toward the opening in the rock. Quinn crawled close behind, holding onto his shirt.

Palms and knees scraping the ground, Nevel and Quinn crawled not fifteen feet through a cavernous tunnel when it suddenly transformed into something else entirely. Nevel held his makeshift torch out before dragging his body behind it. The hot torch was scorching the side of his fist where he held it, forcing Nevel to hold it only by a few dry reeds. Once Nevel was no longer burning his fist, he was able to take in the view with wide eyes. His jaw dropped to the floor.

Inside, the torch exposed an adobe-type clay room three times the size of Nevel's bedroom at home. Turning three hundred and sixty degrees, Nevel saw shelves upon shelves of books stacked neatly inside this clay hideaway. Nevel shook his head and wiped his eyes to make sure he was seeing this clearly. This wasn't the library in his mind, but it was the closest to it he had ever been in reality.

Nevel noticed oil lamps secured to the walls and quickly lit them, happy to be relieved of the fiery torch that was still scorching his fist. Dropping what was left of his torch and stomping on it with his boot, Nevel looked at the room now as the oil lamps exposed its full glory. Behind him, Quinn gasped.

"A depository!" Nevel couldn't believe his eyes. He had heard stories over his lifetime of crow markings and underground tunnels, depositories and rendezvous locations, but Nevel had never actually seen proof.

"A what?! It's magnificent," Quinn gaped. Nevel suspected she was looking at more books than she ever would see in her lifetime.

"I had heard that these large depositories existed throughout Australia—three, actually—all secure and secret locations known only to the higher officials in the U.B.M. They're places where the largest volumes of books are stocked. And they keep changing them; books are switched out of these holding cells as needed, or as demanded."

Nevel walked from one side of the room to another, measuring with his steps and counting in his head. This particular depository was enormous. It must have been the largest of the three; Nevel couldn't imagine another site being larger or in a better hiding place. Nevel surmised that the ceiling was easily twelve feet high as he ran his palms flat against the walls and stared up at it; it was rounded out like their hidden cave, except with no hole in the ceiling. The books were neatly stacked on small wooden bookcases that Nevel thought had to have been assembled within the walls of the hollow. He imagined carpenters at work, sawdust falling on clay. There were four oil lamps built into the walls that easily lit the entire room. They were full of oil; someone made sure to keep this place in top shape. Two wooden chairs sat at either side of an immense wooden table, all probably built inside the room as well. On the table sat a wooden box and there were two stacks of crates on either side of the inner door. The books on the shelves were not covered in dust or dirt. Nevel imagined someone must have to clean this place regularly to keep up the integrity of the books.

"Amazing," Quinn said her voice still breathy

with awe.

Nevel walked over to a crate labeled in chalk hieroglyphs similar to the ones he would see on a market window and, pulling the knife from the pack, cracked it open. Inside, Nevel saw cans of fruits and crackers and bottles of water. A small bit of saliva attempted to pool in his dry mouth and made him feel nauseous. He was hungry from the climb and in this place he felt at home. He didn't think twice about using the resources of the U.B.M.; they had surely used him as a resource over the years. Nevel picked up a can of fruit.

"What are you doing?" Quinn asked. "Stop! Don't! This isn't ours. We'll get in trouble—"

"My parents are U.B.M....don't you think they would want their starving, missing son to eat?" Nevel said as he tore off the top.

"Oh, well, I guess so then," Quinn nervously conceded.

"We're not going to bed hungry tonight." Nevel smiled, forcing open a jar of peaches and dipping his fingers in. He shoveled the sweet fruit into his mouth as fast as he could. He tossed a jar to Quinn, and she did the same.

"I wonder if there's anything here I haven't read." Nevel smiled, looking out at the sea of books spread before them.

"Only one way to find out," Quinn said as they both walked excitedly to the shelves.

It was something he did often in his mind, touching spines like they were gold, scanning titles, so Nevel was in a dreamlike state and had to continue to remind himself that this was, indeed, reality. Nevel stopped a moment and watched Quinn, wondering what it must be like to have so many books at her fingertips after so many years without them (with the exception of the ten minutes a year on Brary Day). He was even a bit envious of her raw reaction.

She ran her long index finger and over the bumps of the spines as she walked slowly along the wall. Every now and then, she would lean in and just smell the bound leather. Quinn finally stopped in her tracks, her arm reached out, almost stroking the book before eventually pulling it carefully from the shelf. She wiped the front cover lovingly with her hand, exposing the embossed words, *Pride and Prejudice*. Quinn didn't even sit; she just stood there smiling as she opened to page one and lost herself in the words.

Nevel pulled his favorite novels from various shelves: *Treasure Island, Moby Dick, Great Expectations, Lord of the Flies,* and *Old Man and the Sea*. He was glad to be reunited with them. He also grabbed titles he had not read to add to his collection, including several espionage novels; maybe they would give him some ideas for escape. Nevel knew that he would be finished with his boastful stack far before she came close to reading half of her book and he shrugged at her as she rolled her eyes. He took them to the floor and settled down to read.

They sat, reading, for what seemed like hours. The silence was broken only when Nevel would get up to reach for a new book. It was peaceful and cool in the depository, the perfect place to get lost in a book. After he'd finished his favorites, Nevel got to work inputting new works with fast darting eyes, a quick thumb flipping page ends, and a focused mind. When his eyes began to sting from the strain, he stood and took a break to stretch.

"I guess you've probably already memorized all the books in here," Quinn noted.

"A lot of them, but I still like to feel the pages of some of my favorites and read them in my hands instead of my head," Nevel said, but as he was speaking he noticed a stack of books set aside that didn't look like the rest.

Nevel moved to the stack of books that had caught his eye. He looked back over his shoulder at Quinn who was once again immersed in her book and, he knew he could act unnoticed.

Nevel pulled one from the stack. The outside was animal hide, and it wasn't professionally bound like the books made during the technology era. Inside, the pages were crisp and somewhat wrinkled. The words were printed neatly by a quill and ink. What was written was nothing he could have imagined.

"Adversaries," Nevel read the title of the first book to himself in disbelief. "Chapter One: Government. Chapter Two: Blane Driscoll."

Suddenly there was hot breath on Nevel's neck and he jumped, closing the book with his thumb marking his place. Quinn was standing next to him.

"What do you have, Bookkeeper?"

"I don't know, logs maybe? They seem to be written by the U.B.M."

"Well, anything interesting in there?"

"There's a...a chapter here on Driscoll."

Quinn shrugged her shoulders and looked at the ground. Then she looked back at Nevel.

"Do you want me to...?"

"Yes, yes...of course," Quinn said, and Nevel wondered if he should read aloud to her as she sat on the ground with her back against the clay wall.

"Blane Driscoll is an adversary of the U.B.M. due to his reception of rewards from the government for illegal acts—acts done for the government, but free of government blame or connection. This results in a long-standing corrupt relationship between Driscoll and the local government. Driscoll and his crew live in Shanty Town. He is considered armed and danger-ous and must be avoided at all costs."

"Lovely," Quinn replied as she stood and walked toward him. "Let's move on, shall we?"

Quinn grabbed the adversaries book from Nevel and began scanning chapters and calling the titles out, "Chief Commander Carrington. Parliamentarians. Maybe something in here can help us escape."

Nevel was already thinking about that. These books may just hold the key to their survival. He picked up another book and opened it carefully. The first crisp page showed simply "Underground Book Movement". As he read each page closely, Nevel was able to put together the pieces he had picked up on from his parents. It was a manual, detailing jobs within the U.B.M., codes, symbols, and protocol. Nevel was mesmerized, reading and memorizing at the same time; occasionally, he would read bits and pieces aloud to Quinn.

"It says the Underground Book Movement is a secret society of vigilant protectors of the world's most valuable commodity: knowledge. It is the belief of the U.B.M. members that knowledge is sacred and should be valued and protected at all costs in order to secure the future generations of humanity." Nevel turned the page, riveted by the information he was absorbing as he continued.

"Listen to this oath: 'I hereby understand the risks involved in the Underground Book Movement and pledge to withhold information about the movement even in cases of blackmail, torture, or threatened death.'" He swallowed a lump as he thought of his parents. He blinked to regain focus and read on. "'I vow to do my duty for humanity in a selfless and ethical way and to expel any selfish motives in my involvement with the underground book movement. I understand that the movement is perpetuating humanity and so I realize my life may be a sacrifice required to do my duty to God, my country, and the world at large.'" Nevel stopped and looked at Quinn. Her eyes were as wide as his.

"You mean this is everywhere? The U.B.M. is worldwide?!" Quinn's eyebrows were furrowed. Nevel brushed the hair off of his forehead and blew the air out of his cheeks through pursed lips.

"I can't believe how much is in here! Here is a part about the crow," Nevel said, tracking the words with his index finger. "Why the crow? It says 'Crows are common like everyday people and are known to be adaptable and intelligent birds. We, too, have had to prove our adaptability since the MegaCrash and we, too, focus on intellectuality. Crows are protective of each other; they often keep watch and alert feeding crows of impending danger.'"

Quinn was leaning over Nevel's shoulder to see what he was reading. Under a crow sketching, Nevel read about how to find the U.B.M. by looking for the mark of the crow, either the bird in its entirety or simply its head or foot, on rocks, walls, and trees. These signified drop off and pick up locations or, in some cases, depositories. Nevel wondered for a moment if he had seen these etchings on trees or rocks before. Flashes of a lifetime of crow images spun through his mind.

"Look at that, Nevel. A secret handshake." Quinn was pointing at a sketch of two hands intertwined, with each person's thumb touching its own index finger. Nevel nodded, knowing now that he had seen that handshake before. He continued to read phrases that conjured up more childhood memories.

"'U.B.M. members can be anywhere, but are always secretive and untrusting. One might note in conversation that they couldn't sleep due to a crow calling outside their window. This is a U.B.M. member identifying him/herself.'" Nevel read on about various jobs within the U.B.M., one specifically drawing his attention; it was the job of the carrier, whose job was to carry the most precious and dangerous books on long journeys, sometimes to other parts of the world. "The pass of the crow" was given to U.B.M. carriers to prove their identities in other territories.

"Amazing!" Quinn looked to Nevel, who was lost in thought.

"It explains so much," Nevel said. He continued

to read until something made him stop short "'Local heads of U.B.M. are D'Artagnan and Elizabeth Bennet.'"

"Who the bloody hell are they? Why does that name sound familiar?" Quinn looked puzzled. Nevel was putting pieces together in his head.

"Because Elizabeth Bennet is in the book you've started reading!" Nevel explained, lost in thought. "The other name is from Dumas."

"Well, how can characters in books be in charge of our local U.B.M.?" Quinn looked to Nevel for answers.

"They're covers, genius!" Nevel's sarcasm sent Quinn's eyes rolling. He didn't notice as he began to realize the crucial part his parents played in the U.B.M. "Wow, I knew my parents were U.B.M., but I didn't realize they were at the head of it here!"

"Your parents are D'Artagnan and Elizabeth Bennet?" Quinn was finally catching on.

"They're their favorite characters," a stunned Nevel stood in silence.

"Wow. That's amazing!" Quinn said. They sat in silence for a moment and then she turned to him. "I don't want to be rude, but I really want to read some more," Quinn hinted and Nevel nodded for her to return to her books. He stood for a long while, scanning and storing all he could learn about the U.B.M. His eyes began to water after several books, and though the next extremely thick book he had his finger on, which had only an embossed letter R on the cover, intrigued him, he decided to give himself a break.

He went and sat at the desk. It felt strange to sit in

a chair after so many days in the outback. It was uncomfortable and seemed impractical now. Still, he sat to examine what was in the box on the desk.

Nevel stroked the smooth birch box with his hand before he carefully slid the top off. Within the box was a thick stack of parchment paper, a pile of quills and a well of ink, and what appeared to be a journal of some sort.

Quinn was still lost in her book, so Nevel opened the journal. It was a log, signed by U.B.M. members, documenting the books that had passed through this depository. He easily found, among other signatures, the signatures of each of his parents. The handwriting was easy to identify, but the names also gave them away; Elizabeth Bennet and D'Artagnan were always side-by-side, and appeared more often than any other names on the pages. He rubbed his fingers across their markings, feeling closer to them than he had in quite some time. Whether they knew it or not, they were still taking care of him—all the way out in the outback. He had been gone long enough now that, despite Nevel's independence and the understanding that they had, his parents would now be worried about him. If they were worried now, how would they feel when he didn't come back at all? Were they even back?

Something out of the corner of his eye caught his attention. From behind one bookcase, he could see a crack. Nevel stood and walked to where the bookcase stood.

Nevel ran his fingers along the long, oval shaped crack that barely showed in the clay. Testing an idea, Nevel slightly pushed on it. His heart fluttered at his success as the portal exposed blackness beyond it. Indeed, it was a small access to somewhere unknown to Nevel. Nevel pushed and peered inside before slowly entering. It was dark inside, and the air was damp. Nevel crouched below the low ceiling and had to squint his eyes to see through the shadows. There was a downward tilt to the tunnel and Nevel imagined the U.B.M. had dug through the rock to create this depository. Surely it connected to the other tunnels left from the Opal miners from decades before. Perhaps it even connected to Nevel's home!

Just as Nevel was about to turn to share the good news with Quinn about their chance for escape, the sound of men's voices echoed through the tunnel.

18

Code

"I am not bloody doin' it, Branson!" one man's voice declared. "I can't believe you would sell out like that!"

And then another chimed in. "We get the Register and we pass it to my guy—"

"You mean the Chief Commander's guy!"

"It'll be a drop, just like the others."

"Yeah, well, how you gonna explain how you got it without selling out the U.B.M.? It's too risky! And I think Walker's onto you. He'll kill you—"

"Not if I kill him first!"

Nevel's heart leapt in his chest. Was this man planning to kill his father? And all over a book!

The men sounded far off, but they must have been on the way to the depository to get the Register. The book Nevel had seen with nothing but the letter R on it must be the Register to which these men were referring! Nevel had heard of a Register before; it was an extremely valuable record of where books were across the world. Nevel jumped back into the depository; his hip banged against the clay door on his way through, causing it to fall closed behind him.

Nevel knew what he had to do. He had to warn his parents and he had to get Quinn out of there quickly. He went back to the table and sat down.

Taking a quill and paper from the box, he set out to leave a note where he knew they would find it; after all, the cave was a place they had been before and surely would return to in the future. Nevel worried about putting his parents' names, even their pseudonyms, on the note. If it fell in the wrong hands, he certainly didn't want to add any unnecessary problems for them. He also didn't want to sign his own name. He knew exactly how to write so they would know it was for them and from him.

He used the code they had made up years ago as a game to play at home in the boredom of memorizing and retaining info. It consisted of the initials of a favorite book followed by numbers, which represented the sequence of words in the third chapter of that book. No one else would have been able to decipher the code.

The book Nevel had chosen to pull from the shelf in his mind was The Last of The Mohicans by Cooper. He knew his parents currently held that copy (at least they still had it when he saw them last). They would be able to use it to decipher the code. He turned to chapter three. He scanned for a word that would help him warn his parents of the men he had overheard. The nineteenth word was "treacherous". He continued to scan to find words that he could string into a sentence to warn his parents. "Men" was the fiftieth word; "awaited" was the seventy-sixth. He continued quickly on, forming the message "Treacherous men await. Leaving the place where we have last seen them with r." He knew they would understand which book the men were after (and consequently which book he would take with him in order to protect it) by simply using the letter "r".

When Nevel was finished, he looked down at the code scratched quickly on the paper. "*TLOTM 19 50 76-ed. 1 38 39 40 41 42 43 44 45 64-in 62apid.*" Nevel signed the note with the word "NOW" and tucked it in the box.

Nevel's initials were fortuitous, his parents always said. Nevel Oswald Walker would be special because his initials spelled NOW. Nevel grabbed the registry off of the table and stashed it quickly in the pack.

"It's getting late," Nevel interrupted Quinn, who was reveling in her book. Come on, we need to move."

"Just a few more minutes," Quinn begged.

"Quinn, we can't stay here forever," Nevel said, although he wished they could.

"Can't we?" Quinn said passively. She still kept her eyes on the book. She didn't notice the urgency with which Nevel was packing up and preparing to leave.

"It's time to decide our fate, Quinn." Nevel said

seriously, grabbing Quinn by the arm to get her attention.

"Why the rush?" Quinn asked, frowning as she yanked her arm free from his grasp.

Nevel closed her book and slid it into the shelf with one hand while pulling her to standing with his other hand. She was angry at his action.

"What do you think you are doing?" Quinn was already pulling at the book that he had just replaced on the shelf.

"Things have recently changed," Nevel said. He pushed the book back onto the shelf and began to blow the oil lanterns out.

"While we were reading? What on earth did you read?" Quinn said angrily as she reached again for the book from where he pushed it on the shelf. Nevel stood in her way. "And what if I'm not bloody ready to leave yet?" Quinn challenged with her hands on her hips.

"Let's just say I read a bit of our future if we stay here, and it is not looking good. We are no longer safe." Nevel grabbed her arm and pulled her toward the door.

"I liked it better when I was the only bad guy," Quinn said, throwing Nevel's hand off of her arm.

"We don't have time for this, Quinn!"

Nevel reached to grab Quinn again. She smacked his hand away with a loud clap that echoed across the clay.

"I'm not leaving, Bookkeeper!" Quinn said, and her nostrils flared.

"You are like a bloody rabid dog frothing at the

mouth. Get a grip! We are in danger here!"

"We are in danger out there, too. We are in bloody danger everywhere we look. Don't you realize I have never had this much time with a real book, not to mention an entire room of them, in my entire life? I am not giving this up just because of a little danger!"

Quinn's words were corrosive, eating away at his heart. He understood what she meant and he wished he could let her stay and read and enjoy what he had been able to enjoy his whole life. He could feel her words tearing away at him, but if he wanted to keep her alive he couldn't give in to her.

"There's a tunnel. I overheard some men. They'll be here any moment and they will kill for what they are after. We have to go now." Nevel stepped back and put his hands up in surrender. "Are you with me or not?"

Quinn's eyes darted to the place where *Pride and Prejudice* was still protruding from the shelf. "I'll go if I can take that book."

"Fine," Nevel said. As soon as she pulled it from the shelf, he blew out the last lantern and pulled her toward the depository exit by her arm, before crawling out in the dark.

On the wet rock ground outside, Nevel used his finger to map out the plan for Quinn. He was rushing, knowing there was someone almost upon them here, but also aware an enemy sat waiting where they were going. The sun was setting fast, and they were running out of light. He tried to remain calm and feign control. "Here is where we will land when we descend," Nevel drew an X next to the large rock he had freehanded.

Next, he drew a circle showing the perimeter around the rock. He drew triangles on every spot where he had seen a campfire. Next, Nevel drew a cone shape projecting out from the X where they would land. There were triangles on either side of the cone.

"We'll tie ourselves together so we aren't separated as we climb down in the dark. Once we hit the ground, we run. We won't be able to speak, not even a whisper. If one of us gets caught, we both go down together," Nevel said, but he knew that if he were caught he would push Quinn to run without him. She would never agree to it now, so there was no sense arguing with her about it while time ticked away.

"This is where we'll be heading." Nevel drew a long wiggly line that looked like a river.

"Is that water?" Quinn asked.

"Yes. Well, it used to be; it's a dry riverbed."

"And beyond it?"

"If we can get to the riverbed and follow it southeast a while, we will get within miles of home." But if he were to tell the truth, Nevel doubted they would ever make it that far.

"And what do we do if we make it home?" Quinn asked. "Everyone will be looking for us now; how do we explain ourselves?"

"I don't know, Quinn. I guess we figure that part out later." Nevel truly did not know. He was stumped, and that's what scared him the most. But they needed to leave. Now.

"Will you promise me one thing, Nevel?" Nevel met her eyes and felt himself drowning in the deep green. "Promise me that if we are captured, you will tell them your only reason for being out here was to help me hide after the charade I pulled at Brary Day. It's about me, Nevel, not you. Promise me you will not tell them you are a bookkeeper, even if you think it may save me."

"I don't make promises to people who take me hostage," Nevel tried to tease, but her eyes stayed locked on his and she did not budge.

"Promise me, Nevel," she commanded.

"Agreed," Nevel said, but not with the sincerity she desired.

"So we just climb down and run?" Quinn asked. "Yep!" Nevel said, "Simple enough, right?" Nevel grabbed her hand and pulled her out to the edge of the ledge. He looked out into the darkness below. Nevel and Quinn stood in silence. Nevel's heart had dropped to his toes. He looped the rope so they were bound together by their belt loops as they prepared for the plunge and run. Quinn squeezed Nevel's hand twice, as if signaling she was ready and that she was with him. Nevel repeated the pattern back to her and then they let go. The very next moment, they were lowering their bodies over the edge.

19
Run

The moon was bright as Nevel and Quinn made their silent descent. Tied together at the waist, they both had to use their hands and feet to slowly lower themselves down. Descending down little by little, the two cringed at every piece of gravel they knocked loose and sent towards the ground and at every limb they brushed against, making more sound than they wanted to.

The wind was on their side this night, blowing and whistling, hiding some of their noises. Nevel was sturdy and confident in his decline, but when their bodies touched, he could feel Quinn shaking as she searched for a foothold. He knew she would never admit weakness, but he positioned himself in hopes he would be able to catch her if she fell. Nevel had to stop and wait for her several times. In the pitch black, he could see flames dancing at campfires surrounding the rock when he looked down. He held his breath on several occasions, freezing still against the rock— and signaling for Quinn to do the same—when he heard the sound of the distant pack of men, surely drinking and joking around their fires.

It was difficult to get alcohol in the post techno-logical era. While it was not illegal, it was a danger-ous trade. People got lost in alcohol after the crash and ended up sacrificing too much at its expense. Nevel knew of a family who had had top-of-the-line farm equipment, and lush vegetables, and their own dairy cow. The father became so reliant on alcohol that he traded every last piece of equipment, and even the cow, to feed his habit. Soon, the family was starv-ing and begging for food in town.

Driscoll's crew was known to make and store their own alcohol, so it was readily available to the gangs of ill doers. Nevel hoped now that they were in-toxicated enough to make their senses weaken and al-low Nevel and Quinn to slip by.

Lowering themselves another twenty feet, they stood still on what Nevel believed to be the final ledge. The noises of the men was louder here, but he hoped the wind was just carrying the voices of a small few and making them sound like more men than were there. In the dark, he just couldn't know how many enemies stood between them and the riverbed.

They climbed the final leg of the journey down until they quietly felt the ground beneath their feet, grabbed hands, and they were off.

Running in the dark was challenging. They hit tree limbs and bushes and stumbled over rocks. The wind was whipping past them and playing tricks on Nevel's ears. He could hear the voices of what sounded like thousands of men hollering at their heels. Nevel's heart beat in his throat, and his breath was fast and choppy. Quinn was faster than Nevel and she pulled ahead, almost breaking their grip. Nevel struggled to keep up, sprinting with every ounce of courage and strength he could muster.

The next sound that registered terrified Nevel. He heard the lashing of sails in the wind and the spinning of wheels on dirt. He cringed at the cranking sound that he knew was fueling the vehicles. The wind rovers were in pursuit. He was out of ideas. No book in his mind could save them now. He ran, thighs pumping, trying to keep up with Quinn. He didn't want to hold her back. He didn't want to hold on to her and keep her in danger. He had to let go.

The clouds parted, and the moon shone down like a beacon on the desert plain where they ran. Quinn and Nevel did their best to escape, ducking and swerving to remain hidden by the blanket of darkness.

They ran with stumbling feet and quickening breaths. Their hands were sweating and their grip slipping. The vehicles' beating sails seemed to be closing in. The panic was causing them to bump into each other more and more, and it was obvious that their plan was slowing them down.

"We have to let go, Quinn," Nevel got out between breaths.

"But—" Quinn gasped out, unable to continue as

she pushed herself even faster.

Now he could hear the gravel crunching beneath the vehicle's wheels, and the spotlight of the moon was revealing them more and more.

"We'll meet at the riverbed," Nevel called and with that, he let go of her hand.

Dropping the weight that had held her back, Quinn now raced swiftly away as Nevel watched, still trying to keep up. He saw a white sail whip by in the direction she was running, and Nevel's heart dropped. He had to do something to throw them off. He turned to run straight into the path of the vehicle, blocking the sight of her.

Wheels screeched, throwing up a cloud of dust and gravel, and the sail thrashed back and forth. Nevel stopped abruptly and held his hands up in surrender. He was panting, frozen in fear, as a brusque voice called out, "Well, what have we here?"

He was caught, but it didn't matter. It allowed Quinn to be free. If they were stopping to capture Nevel, it meant they were no longer chasing after her. Despite his terror, he was relieved.

That was, until he heard the second vehicle whiz by, followed by a third, and a fourth, and a fifth—a fleet of men all heading in her direction. A sack was thrown over Nevel's head, and his hands and feet were tightly bound by a coarse rope. He was lifted up and thrown into the back of the vehicle like luggage. His head hit the metal side, and he passed out cold.

Nevel's head throbbed. He opened his eyes and found himself sitting on a dirt floor inside a shack of some kind. His hands and feet were both tied, but he no longer had the sack over his head. He tilted his head to wipe dripping sweat from his forehead with his bound hands and saw that it wasn't sweat at all, but blood. He remembered every moment leading up to his capture. Swallowing hard, he thought of the white sails that were whipping by after Quinn. She was amazing in the desert. Maybe she got away. He couldn't bear to consider the other possibilities.

Nevel could hear sounds of men not far away. They sounded drunk and seemed to be celebrating. He tried to focus, tried to take in their words to gain some clue as to where he was, but their speech was slurred, and they were too far away to make anything out. Nevel looked around again. It was dark still, but he imagined dawn would be breaking soon. The only reason he could see in the dark shed was because of the streaks of orange moonlight seeping through the cracks in the walls and ceiling. I must be in Shanty Town, he realized.

There were some hay bales scattered about the shed. A bucket, turned on its side, sat next to a rake leaning on the back wall, and a rusty chain hung from the ceiling. He wondered if the chain would be used as a torture device later to get him talking. He swallowed hard. Nevel realized he could make out some images visible in the moonlight through several cracks in the walls. He could see a piece of a front porch that looked weathered and worn. A pile of garbage had been left at the edge of a street, and flies were swarming the mess. All around his shed, he saw buildings similar to his makeshift prison. Nevel wondered if Quinn might be inside one of the dark sheds like he was, but he hoped not. He hoped she was lying under the blanket of stars that spanned the outback and had twinkled over his head last night. She was sure to feel bad about his capture, but he hoped she was smart enough to continue on her own.

From within the drunken slurs of Driscoll's motley crew, Nevel thought he heard a muddled cry. He listened carefully, pressing his ear to a crack, but he could hear nothing but the jeers of the men. He must have imagined it, he thought. But minutes later, he heard it again. This time it was clear and definite.

"Caw!" he heard Quinn call from not thirty yards away. It was weak as it had been before, but this time it did not make him want to laugh. His heart leapt and sank all at once at the sound, and he suddenly felt sick to his stomach.

Nevel forced himself up on his bound feet and hopped to the largest crack in the wall from the side of the shed from which he heard the sound. "No, he told himself, "no. You didn't hear her. It was just—"

"Caw," she called again. His heart sank. It seemed to be coming from a dark shed like his across the street. She sounded like a wounded bird, and it killed him that he could not run to her and help her.

"CAWCAW!" he responded finally. He wanted to sound strong for her. He wanted to remind her that she was strong, too. He hopped along the wall of the shed, crouching and reaching to peer through cracks in the hopes that he would catch a glimpse of her. Nothing.

But still he knew the truth.

They had Quinn. His body sunk to the floor in defeat. He tried not to imagine her wrists raw like his from the rope wrapped tight around them. He tried not to think of the scenarios a beautiful girl like Quinn might face in a place like this, so much worse than any horrors they could inflict upon him. But he couldn't keep his mind from the worry—hands touching her... grabbing...taking...NO! He had to get to her.

Nevel punched the wall with his bound fists.

Who was he kidding? There would be no escaping today.

20

Reveal

The shed door creaked open. The blinding sunlight that poured in exposed his attempts to cut his binding ropes by rubbing them against the spike of a rake. The light prompted Nevel to stop in order to hold up his bound hands as a shield. As his eyes began to adjust, Nevel saw big black boots with metal tips standing just feet in front of him.

Scanning up from the boots were long jeans, leather chaps—with a holster that surely housed both guns and knives—a broad chest covered by a vest, and the red-bearded face anyone would recognize. There was no mistaking him. Blane Driscoll, the Devil of Queensland.

"Get up, boy," Driscoll growled.

Nevel's legs quivered as he stood in front of the

ox of a man they called Driscoll. He wondered if this was it. Was this the moment he would draw his last breath? Would Driscoll shoot him right there or slit his throat? Nevel swallowed a lump in his throat and put his bound hands over his twisting stomach. "Nevel Walker?" Driscoll ordered Nevel to confirm his identity.

"Yes, sir," Nevel answered, realizing now it was just the two of them. That was odd. Surely Driscoll's men would want to witness any punishments issued. Why did he come alone?

"You know we got Quinn?" Driscoll spoke. Nevel's eyes narrowed, but his lips stayed sealed in a tight, defiant line. He wanted to spit in Driscoll's face. How could he let his own daughter suffer at the hands of his raucous men?

Yes, he knew they had Quinn, but Nevel wasn't giving this bastard any information. "No," he replied with a quivering voice as his eyes burned a hole in the floor.

Driscoll's laugh thundered through the shed and echoed off the walls. Nevel squeezed his eyes shut and waited for the moment Driscoll would draw the gun and shoot him through the heart.

"It's OK, son. Don't lose your lunch," Driscoll boomed. "I ain't gonna hurt you right now." Surprised, Nevel looked questioningly at Driscoll. "There's a lot more to this story than you may know, lad," Driscoll said. He motioned for Nevel to sit on a hay bale. Nevel rolled his eyes. "I ain't inviting you to sit. I'm telling you," Driscoll barked. Nevel jumped to sit as he was told. Driscoll closed the shed door and sat on the bale opposite him. "So Quinn wrangled you into helping her escape after her little shenanigans, did she?" he asked.

Driscoll must have talked to Quinn first. This was the story she had wanted to feed them in order to protect Nevel and minimize his involvement.

Nevel rolled his eyes. This wouldn't be his story; he would never give them Quinn. He would sacrifice himself before he would let her take the blame. Beads of sweat were forming on his forehead. He wanted to be the hero in this story, but was he really ready to die for her?

"There's a lot more to the story than you may know, sir," Nevel mimicked, throwing Driscoll's words back in his face.

Driscoll leaned forward, stopping inches from Nevel's nose. "Careful, boy, you wouldn't want to make me mad." His breath smelled of stale smoke and whiskey.

"No, sir, I wouldn't, sir," Nevel said, still wiggling from the scratchy hay.

"Well, then, let's hear it," Driscoll demanded.

The sweat was dripping from Nevel's forehead like rain. He could feel heat rush through his face and he imagined that his ears were as red as fire. He thought of Quinn's weak crow's call and imagined her bound in a shed, with dirty hands pawing at her. He felt sick. "Quinn chased me into the outback and held me hostage," Nevel blurted out.

Driscoll burst into laughter again. He got up from the hay bale and walked around the small shack, snickering and shaking his head in disbelief. "That's fresh, boy, fresh!" he said as he wiped tears from his ruddy cheeks.

"It's true," Nevel protested. He straightened himself to sit up a bit taller on the hay bale, tracking Driscoll's moves around the room as he tried to compose himself. He hadn't considered the thought that Driscoll wouldn't believe the truth. "She was after me for information and—"

"What information?" Driscoll stopped pacing and turned abruptly, returning to Nevel in three long strides. Driscoll leaned in again, and Nevel could feel his prickly beard against his sunburnt cheeks. Driscoll's black eyes flattened, and Nevel feared he had chosen the wrong tactic to save Quinn.

"What information, boy?" Driscoll roared again when Nevel did not answer.

Nevel turned his face away from Driscoll and winced as he continued. "She wanted to know more about who she is."

Driscoll whipped his head around to meet Nevel's eyes again. "And why would she be asking you?" Driscoll bellowed.

"BECAUSE I AM A BOOKKEEPER!"

He had said it. Out loud. The air hung still, as if waiting for Driscoll's response. The man stood and walked away. Nevel blinked and gasped in fresh air, grateful for a relief to Driscoll's rank breath. Nevel's heart pounded in his throat; he waited for a response from Driscoll, but all he could hear was his own racing pulse. He had done it. In one sentence, he may have saved her, but he'd condemned himself in the end.

It was worth it; at least he tried to convince himself that it was. But he worried what it would mean to his parents—who would be brokenhearted to lose their son. Also, the U.B.M. would be put at risk. All the information he had learned in the depository would be tortured out of him. He would have to turn to stone to make himself immune to his imminent demise.

Finally, Driscoll broke the silence. "You are awfully brave for a young lad. Reminds me of someone I used to know." Nevel sat and hung his head, staring at the dirt floor.

Nevel didn't dare utter another word. He just sat still, like a statue, frozen under the weight of the revelation. It was done now; it was over. He had set his fate and would accept all that came with it. He felt numb. His eyes no longer welled with tears, but were now made of glass; his heart had turned to stone.

Driscoll walked toward him and crouched down, tilting his head to try to meet Nevel face to face again. Nevel turned the other way.

"You got feelings for her?" Driscoll asked, his voice not-so-booming now as it had been before.

Nevel did not speak. His tongue had shriveled. His mouth felt sewn shut. He refused to give Driscoll anything more. After a moment, Driscoll sighed, and then stood and walked away.

"And I suppose you gave her the answer she was looking for?" Driscoll asked. He was at the door, and Nevel hoped he would just leave. "Well, she must have some feelings for you, too, because she lied for you," Driscoll said from the doorway, his back to

Nevel. Nevel lifted his hung head to look at Quinn's father, who stood motionless, his hand on the door handle. "Can you believe that? My own daughter lying right to my face?" Driscoll turned and met Nevel's stare. He knew.

Nevel looked at the crack in the wall that faced Quinn's shed. It was quiet now. Had Driscoll let her go? Nevel swallowed hard, realizing that he might have gotten out of this situation without him sacrificing himself, and risking the lives of others. Maybe Driscoll had never planned to hurt Quinn. But what did it matter now? He had already given himself away. It was too late.

Driscoll opened the shed door slowly. He stopped for a moment, his shadow spilling across the dirt floor to Nevel's feet, and then walked out and slammed the door closed behind him.

Judging by the hunger brewing in his belly and the slow change of the sunrays spilling into the shed, Nevel guessed it was late afternoon when the door opened again.

The light poured in, blinding him. This time he did not shield his eyes or cower to its harshness. He sat and stared straight into the bright light, ready to face whatever was coming.

Driscoll's immense silhouette was black against the light. He moved toward Nevel with a long knife. Nevel winced as Driscoll bent down and sawed the ropes apart, freeing his feet.

"Let's go," Driscoll demanded. Nevel stood and followed him through the shed door.

160

21

Clean

As he walked down the dusty, red dirt road lined by graffiti-covered shacks, Nevel knew he had guessed right; he was in Shanty Town. His hands were still bound in front of him, and his wrists were rubbed raw by the rope. Nevel walked in Driscoll's shadow past the sheds he had peered at through the cracks. His eyes ran over each building as he passed, looking for some sign of Quinn. He wanted to call for her, but he worried it would just draw attention. It was quiet now. He hoped that meant she was asleep, or better yet, gone—released.

They passed porches full of jeering men drinking out of cans, and a few groups messing about in the street with various pieces of junk; but on the whole, Shanty Town was eerily quiet. No one dared speak to or approach Driscoll unless he called upon them to do so. Nevel could tell Driscoll's presence was a heavy one here, and it made him even more frightened for himself and for Quinn.

At the end of the long dusty street, Driscoll turned and climbed the front porch steps to a blue clapboard house. Nevel followed without objection. He was in too deep to try anything risky now.

The floors were wooden and creaked under their steps. Driscoll opened the front door and led Nevel into an entryway, which opened to a living room on the right and had a long hallway leading straight back. It was clearly a home, and a surprisingly nice one for this area. The walls were clean and white and were framed by a pale green molding. The floors were polished oak. A wooden rocking chair sat empty by a fireplace in the living room, and on the other end of the room sat a long wooden bench covered by pillows and a patchwork quilt. Nevel wondered where in the world he was. He followed Driscoll down the hallway and was surprised to see a picture hanging on the wall. It was a sketch of Driscoll's rough profile looking out over a sea of shacks. Nevel blinked twice, stunned. This was Driscoll's house.

"Clean yourself up and put on those clothes. You've got thirty minutes," Driscoll said gruffly when they reached a door at the end of the hall. With a sharp yank of his knife, he cut the ropes binding Nevel's hands, before pushing in Nevel into the room and walking away.

Nevel rubbed his wrists, which were bright red and blistered from the coarse rope, and looked around the stark room. Like the rest of the house, the walls were white, framed by green molding, and the floors were the same polished wood. In the corner of the room was a washtub and a wooden chair with a green towel folded neatly over the back. There was a small bed with a white lace covering under the window. On the bed were some gray pants and a white shirt that had been laid out for him. For a moment, Nevel held back tears at the thought of his old bedroom and the fact that he would never see it again.

He forced the thoughts from his mind and soldiered on to the task at hand. The washtub was filled with cool water, and Nevel cupped his hands to drink from it before climbing in. He took off the clothes he had worn for so many days now; they practically disintegrated as he shed them and dropped them in a pile of red dust to the floor. He stepped gingerly into the tub and sank into the water, basking in the soothing, wet luxury he had been without for so many days. As he cupped his hands and poured the water over himself, red dirt melted from his skin and into the water. He grabbed the bar of soap and began to scrub the dirt away; first from his blistered feet, then his tight muscular legs and arms, and finally his crusted face and tangled hair. He ducked beneath the surface several times, relishing the cool water. His skin slowly changed from the aboriginal red that had covered him to the tanned bronze he had known before this great adventure began.

After cleaning every nook and cranny, Nevel stood and toweled himself dry. He realized now, he had forgotten his pain and fears, at least temporarily.

Now, as he wiped away the last hint of dirt from his skin, his worries returned. What had happened to Quinn? Had they let her go, or was she suffering here somewhere? What would become of his parents? What would happen to him?

He dressed in the plain, pressed white button up shirt that was clean and stiff. It was big on Nevel—Driscoll's, no doubt—and he had to roll the cuffs several times before his hands were free. The grey slacks were thin from wear, but were clean and soft and fit surprisingly well. Nevel imagined Driscoll must have taken these from someone else—a victim?—because Nevel would never have fit in Driscoll's clothes. He hoped he wasn't wearing a dead man's pants and shuttered at the thought, quickly trying to squelch it from his mind. Nevel put his own boots back on and laced them tight, wincing as the blisters rubbed against the leather and opened again. Then he sat on the bed and waited, trying to sooth his fears by rereading that one line in the poem he had read for Quinn just days ago; "In the mud and scum of things, there always something sings."

The sound of footsteps in the hall startled Nevel, and he stood as the door opened.

"Let's go," Driscoll ordered. Nevel followed him nervously out of the room and down the hall toward the front of the house. They entered the dining room, where a long, large oak table was covered with food and fine china and was set for three.

"Sit," Driscoll commanded. Nevel obliged, taking the spot on the side nearest the door. His mouth immediately started watering at the breads and meats laid out in front of him; but his stomach was twisting, and his heart was racing.

Driscoll walked out of the room and down another hallway. Nevel eyed the food warily, wondering if it was poisoned, or if this was his last meal before his execution. His pondering was interrupted by the echoing sounds of footsteps heading toward the room where he waited. Nevel couldn't imagine who the third guest was. He watched as Driscoll returned to the room, but his eyes widened and he started to stand as he saw who followed close behind.

"Stay in your seat!" Driscoll barked.

Quinn stepped out from behind her father. She, too, was clean and in new clothes. Her long, red hair had been brushed smooth and hung, gleaming, down her back, and a white eyelet gown fell to her toes. She was beautiful. Nevel gaped at the sight of her, but he quickly looked to her eyes to see if she was OK. She looked scared, like Nevel, but the light was still in her eyes. Nevel sighed in relief.

Driscoll sat at the head of the table and motioned for Quinn to take the seat opposite of Nevel.

"Eat!" he ordered. Quinn looked to Nevel and he knew she was probably wondering the same thing he was. Was it poisoned?

Driscoll tore a leg off the roasted chicken and began eating ravenously, like a wild dog. Nevel decided it must be safe, so he pulled off a wing and bit into the tender flesh. Quinn followed his lead. Nevel drank water from his pewter goblet only after Driscoll did, and Quinn did the same.

Driscoll ate in pensive silence, and Nevel didn't

dare try to talk to Quinn. Nevel eyed her closely, looking for any sign of injury; Quinn seemed to be doing the same. Finally, after what seemed like hours, Driscoll spoke.

"You two have put me in a difficult situation. It ain't one I've been in." Nevel was surprised to see that Driscoll seemed nervous. He continued. "I am an outlaw, a man of steel and grit, but I once knew love."

Quinn blinked twice. Nevel watched her for more of a reaction, but she was staring down at her plate.

"Her name was Rose. We married without making a big deal of it, so no one knew. Her family detested me. I can't say as I blame 'em; she was too good for me. I didn't want her to have to stoop to living with the scum of my neck of the woods. So I got her a house in town and took care of her from a distance. I lived here, in this house, and secretly visited her. We had a beautiful baby we named Quinn, after Rose's mother." Driscoll looked at Quinn. She swallowed and did not look up to meet his gaze.

"Rose was a nurse, a respectable woman. But she loved me and so she tolerated my garbage." Driscoll looked out the window for a moment before turning back to Quinn.

"You look like her," he said and he cleared his throat and looked out the window again. "She was beautiful."

Nevel watched Quinn look up from her plate finally and at Driscoll. Her eyes were pooling with tears, but Nevel could tell she was doing everything she could to keep them from spilling over.

"Quinn...er...you were a happy child; active and

always into mischief. Like me," he said almost proudly. Driscoll grabbed a roll and slathered it with butter. He offered it to Quinn, who was staring at him; but she shook her head. "Rose got sick. Dr. Dudley did everything he could." Driscoll looked at Quinn at the mention of Dr. Dudley, and their eyes met for the first time. He cleared his throat again. The tears in Quinn's eyes spilled over, but she remained silent. Nevel shifted in his seat as Driscoll continued. "When she died, I went on a rampage. I had no business raising a child. I didn't want you to live the terrible life I did, and so The Dudley's took you. But I have always been near and I have watched you grow. No one could ever touch you; I wouldn't have it."

Nevel's mind raced. He was happy at first. This meant Quinn would be OK. Driscoll was actually protecting her! But then, it sunk in. He had sacrificed himself, his family, and the U.B.M. And for what?

Driscoll broke Nevel's thoughts as he spoke again. "When you two took off over a week ago, I knew about Quinn's charade at Brary Day. I knew Bull would want his revenge and so I had Bull killed." Nevel and Quinn swallowed hard. "Problem was, once you were both missing, it started to look bad. With them postings up, people were looking for funny business. The talk started around town that only a bookkeeper would go hiding. And, well, you two were both gone, so everybody started pointed fingers at ya. I sent my guys out to pick you both up. Told 'em one of you had to be the bookkeeper, and we were goin' to find out which one to get our reward. And so they brought you both to me and now I see that there is—

like the lad so boldly said—more to the story than even I knew."

Quinn and Nevel looked at each other from across the table. Quinn glared at Nevel accusingly, angered at the prospect that he had given away his secret. "I don't know what you mean," she said, and her voice cracked.

"I told him," Nevel said, stopping her from whatever story she might have planned.

"Told him what?" Quinn angrily asked.

"I know your boy here is a bookkeeper," Driscoll revealed nonchalantly between bites.

"He's not!" Quinn asserted, "I am!"

"Ha! Fresh!" Driscoll replied.

"Quinn, don't..." Nevel was touched, but he wasn't going to allow her to throw herself into this mess

"I...I keep all the books in my mind on shelves." Quinn was direct and intense. She looked Driscoll right in the eyes without flinching. She didn't sound like a liar. "I have read every book in the library and memorized them. My father has connections; I have been to the library more than just on Brary Day. My whole life, I've been collecting info and—"

"She's lying!" Nevel was furious.

"Well, there you are, lad. If you were the bookkeeper, how would you have gotten books to memorize? You don't exactly have connections. She's got an edge on ya," Driscoll said around a mouthful of fried potatoes.

"I...I..." Nevel tried to start but he couldn't tell Driscoll without giving up the U.B.M. He was astonished. She had thought of this already! She knew he would have to protect his parents and the U.B.M.

"Well, now, you got me in a mess," was all Driscoll said. "My daughter, a bookkeeper? Hmm. The town's been a buzz guessing just that, but I couldn't believe it." Driscoll seemed to be thinking out loud. "Now, I'm gonna have to turn Nevel here into the government. Don't see a way around it. They think one of you is the bookkeeper, and I ain't givin' 'em Quinn."

"Take me," Nevel said. He was happy to once again have Quinn off the chopping block.

"But, they won't believe it!" Quinn cried. "They know it's me! I am the bookkeeper! I am! It is the only thing that makes sense. I am the bookkeeper and I forced him to help me survive in the outback while I tried to hide. I fled after the posters caused so much of a buzz. I knew they'd figure it out. Don't give him to them! I won't let you! I will turn myself in, too. You won't be able to stop me!" Quinn had tears in her eyes now again as she pleaded.

Nevel was terrified. Why was she doing this? She didn't have to do this.

For the first time, Driscoll looked almost... scared. "I won't have you killed. I'm giving them Nevel," Driscoll reiterated.

"They'll test him. He'll never pass, and then they'll come after me anyway." Quinn argued, rising from her seat to stare her father down.

"I'll pass!" Nevel slammed his hand down on the table, rattling the dishes.

"How?" Driscoll said between bites, with a

mouthful of food, "She's right! I know your reputation. I asked around. No one thinks you could be the bookkeeper."

Nevel was silenced again and swallowed hard. How did Quinn always defeat him?

She sat back down; her cheeks were a pale white, but she held her head high as she faced Driscoll. "There has to be a bloody way out of this."

"Damn, you are feisty! You get it honest," Driscoll said shaking his head, "we may have to try something else entirely."

"Like what?" Nevel asked, his face still hot with anger.

Driscoll dropped the last bone he was sucking on onto his plate and wiped his mouth with the back of his hand. "We could fake everyone out and pretend to kill you both off."

Nevel felt a huge sense of relief. In this plan, he actually had a chance to live.

"You would have to completely disappear," Driscoll went on, "and I can't help you with that. I could get you to the edge of town just before sunrise tomorrow, but after that you'd be on your own. I'll spread word that you died while I was capturing you—fell off the rock or something." He looked at them both sternly.

"We can disappear," Quinn said, looking at Nevel after taking a deep breath in.

"Yes," Nevel reassured her. "We will disappear." "You'll need tonight to plan. I'll wake you before dawn." Driscoll got up and stomped toward the front porch with a jug of whiskey, leaving the two alone.

As the front door slammed shut behind him, Quinn hopped up from the table and ran to Nevel. He met her halfway and wrapped her tightly in his arms. After a moment, he reluctantly let her go. They looked toward the porch to make sure Driscoll wasn't about to protest; he was chugging whiskey in a rocking chair with his back to the house. Nevel grabbed her hand and dragged her to the room where he had changed earlier. With a quick glance over his shoulder towards the front door, he pulled her inside.

22

Request

"Well, what's the plan?" Quinn asked as Nevel pulled the door closed tight behind them.

Nevel didn't reply; instead, he grabbed her around the waist and pulled her close to him. He looked her in the eyes and slowly leaned in to kiss her. Quinn closed her eyes and fell into the kiss, wrapping her hands around the back of his neck. Nevel's skin felt electrified at her touch. Her lips were so soft. His heart pounded so hard against his chest, and he felt like it would explode. When Nevel finally pulled away, he watched her eyes slowly flutter open, a wide smile gracing her face.

"That was some trick you pulled in there. I can't believe you!" Nevel chastised Quinn who still seemed to be regaining her composure after the kiss. She tucked her hair behind her ears and stepped away from him.

"We agreed in the outback that we would stick together!" Quinn responded. "I wasn't going to let you go down like that. This way Driscoll will save both of us; see, it all worked out. So now, what's your plan for our disappearing act?"

Nevel rolled his eyes, but then grinned. "We join the U.B.M. I memorized everything there is to know about it in the depository. We can travel and carry important books to different places and..." Nevel trailed off. He was so lost in the thought of a life free from the secrecy he'd always known that he hadn't stopped to wonder if this was really what Quinn wanted. He put his hands on her shoulders and looked her in the eyes. "This is the rest of our lives, Quinn. Do you really want to uproot yourself and give up everything just to be with me? You can still be you here. Driscoll can fix it by turning me in." Nevel knew he was coming on intensely, but he had to be honest and make sure she heard and understood every word.

"I've already trusted you with my life, Bookkeeper." Quinn met his stare. "We didn't know if we would live or die when we dropped from that big rock together, remember? But we did it, and here we are." Quinn turned her palms up and shrugged. "We have a chance at something amazing now with the U.B.M., something our friends would never have a chance at. Neither of us is doing anything here. We're just taking up space. In the outback, we both saw that we are meant for greater adventures. I want to do this. I want to do this with you," Quinn pleaded.

Nevel wrapped his arms around Quinn. He was planning in his head. The first order of business with the U.B.M. would certainly involve the Register. Suddenly he felt sick. "Quinn," he said harshly as he pulled away. She looked at him, confused. "The pack! Where is the pack?"

"Oh...um...well, you were wearing it when we were captured. I'm sure that Driscoll's guys have already searched through it and taken what they wanted." Quinn sat on the edge of the bed and crossed her legs. "Why are you so worried? Is it because I had that Jane Austin book in there? I am sure that's gone now. Sorry, I made you lose it—"

"No!" Nevel cut her off. "There was another book in the pack. I didn't tell you about it, but it... it's hugely important to the U.B.M." Nevel paced the room, tugging at the curls that fell against his forehead. "What have I done?"

"Nevel, I am sure it's OK." Quinn clearly didn't grasp the magnitude of the situation.

Nevel couldn't believe he may have lost the Register. He rounded on Quinn. "We've got to go see Driscoll," he said urgently. "I have to ask for the pack, and we have to tell him that we need to leave tonight, just for a bit, so we can see my parents."

"He'll never go for that; it's too risky. And besides, he probably doesn't even know there was a pack." Quinn placed her hand in the center of Nevel's back.

"Come on," Nevel said. He grabbed her hand and, before she had time to react, had dragged her down the hall to the front door. Through the window, they could see Driscoll slumped in a rocking chair, the jug of whiskey tipped to his lips. This is risky, Nevel thought to himself, disturbing an outlaw while he's been drinking. But Nevel knew he had no choice. Reluctantly pushing the front door open, Nevel slipped out to the porch and approached the red-faced Driscoll, careful not to sneak up on him. Quinn cowered behind Nevel.

"I need my pack," Nevel said matter-of-factly, which seemed to catch Driscoll off guard anyway.

"Your what? What the hell—" Driscoll stood from his chair and took one thundering step towards Nevel.

Nevel refused to cower. "I had a backpack on when I was captured and I need it back." Nevel stood tall, puffing out his chest and tipping his head up to look into the man's face. Maybe if he acted like a man, he would be given the respect of a man.

Driscoll looked at Nevel and laughed a bit before sitting back down in his chair and taking another gulp of whiskey. "It's in the closet in your room, boy."

Nevel felt like an idiot. When it was clear Driscoll was no longer paying any attention to them, he and Quinn raced back into his room and opened the closet. Sure enough, the pack sat on the floor just inside. Nevel quickly checked the pockets and was relieved to find that everything was still in it.

"Wow, Driscoll really has his men under control if they turned you in pack and all!" Quinn said as she pulled out her boots and tugged them on. Grabbing a towel, she wiped them clean. The bright pink snakeskin and steel toes peaked out below the hem of her dress.

Nevel was impatient to get moving. Just because the book was still safely stowed in the pack didn't mean the men hadn't seen it. "Come on," he said, grabbing Quinn by the arm again and pulling her toward the door.

Quinn shook his hand off of her arm. "I'm not a bloody ragdoll, Nevel. Quit pulling me around and tell me what's going on!"

Nevel felt bad; she was right. He stopped and turned to her, offering his hand instead of taking hers. "I'm sorry," he said. "I need to remind myself to let you in on the info in my head, but I'm used to keeping secrets, and we just don't have any time right now. I don't mean to keep you in the dark. I will always tell you everything, I promise. For now, though, time is ticking." She smiled and gave him her hand. This time she surprised him by pulling him in for a long, deep kiss. Nevel lost himself in her embrace; he ran his hands through her hair and stepped closer to her only to have her step back. He stepped again and again, and so did she, until he had backed her against the wall. After a few moments, the kiss slowed to soft pecks. As Nevel caught his breath and pulled back from Quinn, he whispered, "Remind me why I ever ran from you?"

She giggled and turned to the window, smoothing her hair down with her hands and straightening her dress.

Nevel ran his fingers through his hair and tried to focus. "We have to go to my house," he told Quinn. We can run there and be back in no time. I believe you know the way." Nevel smirked. "My parents can tell us where to drop into a tunnel once Driscoll lets us go." He knew there were tunnels from his house, but he couldn't risk bumping into anyone locally who would know them. They would have to start outside of town, where they would be strangers to everyone.

"He'll never go for it," Quinn said, turning now from the window to look at him.

"He's been drinking enough now that he may not even notice," Nevel said.

"And what if someone sees us?"

"I don't know. We can hide." Nevel tugged at his hair. "We don't have a choice. The whole town's asleep; we've gotta go while we have the chance. There's just no way around it." He put on the pack and offered her his hand. "I'll get to see my parents. Do you want to see your...er...Dr. Dudley?" Nevel wasn't sure how to refer to the man who had raised Quinn as his own daughter.

"He'll have to mourn with the others when he hears I'm dead." Quinn's harsh words seemed to surprise even her. She started again, "I mean, no. I don't want to see him. I can't bear to watch him get any sadder than he already is. I'm sure Driscoll will tell him the truth. They obviously go way back."

Nevel tightened the laces on his boots. "You never did tell me why he was so sad," he said, watching her out of the corner of his eye.

"He lost the love of his life," she replied softly. "My mum died of cancer soon after the MegaCrash; at least we assumed it was cancer. He was an oncologist before, you know?" Quinn looked to the window, and Nevel suspected she was watching the stars.

"Oh, man, I'm sorry. I guess he could have saved her."

"Who knows? Plenty of people still died from cancer before the MegaCrash, even with the best technology, but I guess if you knew there was a chance you could have saved the love of your life... well, I guess I'd be sad, too. It was just hard because I didn't just lose my mum; I lost him, too. And then I find out, years later, that neither of them was mine to begin with."

Nevel didn't know what to say. He pulled her into a tight hug, and she buried her face in his hair for a moment before pulling away. She took a deep breath and grabbed his hand.

"Come on," she said. "Let's go see your parents and find out where the tunnels are."

Nevel smiled and they walked hand in hand to the porch.

"You again?" Driscoll's speech was slurred.

"We have to pop out just for a bit. Just to get ready for tomorrow. We've made our plans. We won't be long, promise." Quinn's voice sounded light and unassuming. Perfect, Nevel thought.

Driscoll grunted, "Uh-huh," before slumping back against the chair. His eyes were closed, and he quickly nodded off to sleep.

Nevel and Quinn looked around at the empty street and took their chance to run.

23

Goodbye

The run through downtown Morgan Creek in the pitch black of night was eerie. In Shanty Town, the sounds of drinking and carrying on still came from within shacks as Quinn and Nevel passed, but the closer they got to Morgan Creek, the quieter and darker it became. The only sounds Nevel could hear were their heavy breaths and the slapping of their boots against the pavement. Nevel had become so accustomed to running that his muscular legs easily carried him on his way. He could now keep pace with Quinn as they ran side by side towards his home.

Soon the road gave way to dirt and Nevel pushed himself to run faster, knowing that in no time, he would be home. His heart dropped to the pit of his stomach. He had ached to return home, and now he feared this would be his last visit; he didn't even know if his parents would be there to say goodbye.

Tank barked from inside the house as they slipped around the side and arrived at the back sliding glass door. Nevel had barely slid the door open to squeeze through when Tank came barreling down the hallway, knocking Nevel to the ground. Nevel let out a quiet, nervous laugh as he rolled out from under the dog's weight, and so did Quinn.

"I missed you, too, buddy," he whispered, rubbing the dog's ears as he was swatted over and over again by his wagging tail. He would miss this.

Nevel got up and brushed himself off. Quinn followed him quietly into the dark house. Nevel motioned for Quinn to sit on the couch and wait; Tank sniffed her boots as she sat.

Nevel went down the hall and turned the bedroom door with caution. He didn't want to knock and scare them; he thought he would be better off whispering to wake them in his familiar voice. As he cracked the door slowly open, he saw his mum asleep in her bed and he smiled. But where was his dad? Nevel stepped inside the bedroom. Suddenly there was a gun to his head.

"Dad, it's me," Nevel whispered and the muzzle fell from his temple.

"Nevel!" His dad cried hoarsely, wrapping his arms around him. At the noise, his mother woke and jumped out of bed in her nightgown to rush to Nevel, hugging him tight and kissing his head. His mother was crying, and Nevel felt her tears hitting his neck—which was still hot and sweaty from the run—as she held him tightly to her chest.

His dad lit a small candle. "Let me get a look at you."

"You're safe!" his mother cried, "Thank God you're safe!" She cradled his face with her hands and looked him over, pulling his arms out to the side with her hands as if to make sure he was all in one piece. "Well, for this moment, at least," Nevel said.

"What do you mean? Are you OK? Where have you been? Oh, Nevel!" His mum pulled him into her arms again, hugging him so tightly he could hardly breathe. Nevel pulled himself away to get her attention.

"I'll tell you everything," he promised. He placed his hands on her shoulders, wrapping his fingers around them to hold her firmly in place, and he tried to keep his voice calm. "Just give me the chance." He had missed her, too, but he didn't have a lot of time.

"You know anything about the other girl who has been missing?" his dad chimed in. "People think she is the bookkeeper." His father backed off of him a bit too now to listen to what he was saying.

"Yes," Nevel said as his mother continued to try to brush the hair off of his forehead and his father kept a hand on his shoulder.

"You were with the girl?" His father continued to get caught up to speed. "What's her name...Quinn?"

"Yes, she's in the living room right now," Nevel tried to interject, but he could barely get a word in.

"Does she know she is suspected to be the bookkeeper?" his dad continued.

"Yes, Dad, yes. Let me tell you everything,"

Nevel begged, "Put on your robes and meet us in the living room."

After brief introductions in the living room, they all sat by candlelight to talk. Nevel and his mother sat on the couch. Quinn sat in a wooden chair that backed up to the window and faced the couch. Nevel's father paced a bit before sitting on the other side of Nevel on the couch. Nevel's mother would not let go of him, wiping her tears every few moments and brushing his hair away from his face dotingly.

"Quinn figured out I was a bookkeeper and chased me into the outback, where she held me hostage." It sounded funny now coming out of his mouth, and he and Quinn couldn't help but smirk a bit. His parents did not seem amused at all. Nevel continued. "I didn't know if she worked for Driscoll or the government, and you all had been gone longer than usual so I didn't know if something had gone wrong. It turned out she just wanted some information from me."

"We got caught up with a drop, that's all. I figured you would know that," Nevel's father said as he got up from the couch and paced the room, stopping to look at Quinn. "What kind of information were you looking for?"

"I was adopted," Quinn answered, "and he was my only chance at finding out who my real parents were. I didn't hurt him; I didn't ever plan to. I'm sorry for the scare."

Nevel's mother glared at Quinn from her seat next to Nevel on the couch. Quinn shifted a bit in her chair.

"So, once I gave her the information," Nevel continued, "we thought it was over. Until we realized someone was after us. I guess you could say we teamed up and ran together from Driscoll's crew until getting captured."

"Captured! By Driscoll?" His mother cupped her hand over her own mouth to try to keep from crying. "How in the world did you get away?"

"Well, we haven't actually gotten away," Nevel said, looking out the window towards the distant lights of Shanty Town. "Driscoll is waiting for us."

"Where?" Nevel's dad was at the window, pulling back the burlap drape to search the lawn for Driscoll's figure.

"He's not here, now, Dad. He...well, I guess you can say he's trusting us to return," Nevel said. "It turns out that Quinn's biological father is Driscoll."

His mother gasped again, and she looked Quinn up and down again, her face wrinkled with distrust.

"It's OK, Mum." Nevel said as he put a hand on his mother's knee. "Driscoll is the one who let us come here tonight to say goodbye."

"Goodbye?" His mother said as she looked across the room at his silent father. His parents appeared absolutely terrified. Tears welled in his mother's eyes, and she pulled Nevel to her chest again. "No, no, no," she muttered into his ear.

"What do you mean, goodbye?" his father asked with a look of worry on his face.

"Driscoll is going to fake our deaths." Nevel said and then he stood and walked toward his father. "He was going to turn us in, but he is letting us live because Quinn is his daughter." His father crossed his arms across his chest. Nevel looked him square in the eyes, searching for approval. "We told him we would disappear. I figured we could join the U.B.M. We can drop in a tunnel out of town and go from there. We need you to tell us where that is. This way, maybe I'll be able to see you again, stay in touch, be of use."

Nevel's dad paced from one end of the room to other and back again, stopping to look out the window each time he passed; he seemed to be working out a plan in his mind. Nevel's mother turned and looked at Quinn, tears streaming down her face. "We wouldn't have to say goodbye if you hadn't done this!" his mother accused, her voice thick with tears.

"If it wasn't Quinn, it would have been someone else, Mum!" Nevel moved back across the room to his mother and sat back down beside her on the couch. "Someone would have figured it out eventually! Don't blame her! We are lucky there is a way to go on and still be in touch." Nevel put his arm on his mother's shoulder and she hung her head and cried.

Quinn tried to speak up. "I never meant for any of this to happen. I'm sorry. I care about Nevel. I promise I wouldn't let him—"

"It's not your fault; it's ours," Nevel's mother quietly spoke, a sound of defeat in her tone. "We should have told our secret from the beginning. The government would have used you for every inch you could give, but they would have kept you alive and safe, and then we wouldn't be forced to say goodbye." She lifted her hung head and turned to look at Nevel now. "I am so sorry, baby. I am so sorry. I thought it was for the best. I thought it was your only chance at a normal childhood. And now, I...I have to let you go too soon..."

"It's OK, Mum. You made the right choice." He put his arm around her. "I wouldn't change a thing. I would never have been able to live as a bookkeeper inside the government walls; you know they make it look so great, but it would have been torture. I would have been watched at all times. I wouldn't have had these wide-open spaces; my bike rides, my afternoons to lie out back with Tank, doing nothing at all. This is exactly the life I would have chosen again and again. Don't apologize. It's OK. I'll be OK."

Nevel's eyes stung from the fresh wave of tears. He didn't want to cry in front of Quinn. He tried to keep it in, but this was the first time his family had ever spoken so openly and honestly about the choices they had made about his life. Wounds from a lifetime of holding a secret were raw and tender, and emotions he had held in his whole life were finally beginning to surface.

His dad sat beside him on the couch and patted his knee. Nevel stood up abruptly and turned to face them, his back to Quinn. He could no longer keep the pot from boiling over. It was time for Nevel to speak the truth. It was time for him to take hold of his life. "I am glad you kept it a secret and kept me isolated all these years, but I am done with it now. I couldn't do it anymore, even if Quinn had not figured out I am a Bookkeeper." A single tear slid down his cheek as he looked at his parents. "I am ready to become a part of this world. I don't want to hide anymore. I want to go make my mark on the world."

A long silence filled the room, broken only by

Mrs. Walker's sniffling and the pounding of Nevel's heart in his ears.

"You're right, Nevel," his dad said as he took his mother's hand. "It's the only way."

Nevel's mother drew in a deep breath and looked up at her son admiringly. "You've grown up a lot this week. I can see it in your eyes. I am going to miss you every second of every day."

Nevel's father stood and pulled him into his arms. "I am proud of you, son; I have always been proud of you. I wish it could be different. I wish we could be together..." His tears were leaking from his eyes.

"We can keep in touch via the U.B.M.," Nevel assured his parents as he began to regain composure and pull away from their embrace. "It is the best we can hope for. And besides, I have Quinn." He paused and looked back at Quinn, who was rising from her chair, before turning back to his mum and dad. "We'll be OK."

"Have Driscoll drop you on the west side of the county line," his father directed. "There is an orchard there with a long stone wall. Look for the sign of the crow; it's along the first section. You'll find a tunnel entrance under a large stone on the ground beneath the crow's feet." His father looked at him straight-faced. "Good luck, son."

Nevel and Quinn walked to the door.

Looking over his shoulder, he smiled at his parents one last time and recited the phrase he had heard so often in his sixteen years. "Look to the moon, look to the sky, at the crow's call, it's time to fly!"

When Tank ran out the back door with them as

they turned to leave, Nevel asked Quinn to give him just one minute to say goodbye to his dog. Quinn obliged and went around front to wait. Nevel wrapped his arms around Tank and whispered, "I love you, boy. Take care of Mum and Dad. Maybe someday we'll see each other again."

Nevel's eyes were blurry from the tears he could no longer stop from coming. His breath was choppy from the sobs. Nevel wrapped both arms around his dog and cried into his thick black fur. The dog licked his salty tears and wagged his tail unknowingly. Nevel patted him one last time on the head and stood to go. Tank cocked his head to the right and whimpered a bit, as if to say "you're leaving again?" He started to follow, and Nevel choked the words out as he commanded, "No, stay." It was too much. He wasn't saying goodbye to just a dog; Tank was his brother, his best friend...the only one who had ever been there for Nevel, no matter what. Finally, Nevel took a deep breath, wiped his eyes, and walked away.

Sniffling, Nevel realized he had forgotten something important. He pulled the Register out of the pack and quickly scanned the pages into his brain by the light of the moon. His parents stood inside the sliding glass door with Tank between them, and he ran back to hand them the book. "I almost forgot! I took this from the depository." Nevel spoke quickly as he handed it to them through the door. "There were some men after it. They sounded dangerous, they mentioned you..." Nevel couldn't bear to tell his father about the death threat. "Anyway, goodbye." Nevel couldn't bear any more heartache, and so he turned and ran away without giving them a chance to respond.

Nevel and Quinn ran back towards town. When their shoes were again on asphalt and they began to pass through the wealthy part of town, Nevel noticed Quinn seemed to slow a bit and he wondered if they were near her home. He wondered if she regretted not saying goodbye to Dr. Dudley, or leaving her life behind in the first place. Now she was tied to an outlaw and a fugitive bookkeeper. Nevel wished, for a moment—for her sake—that she was just a prissy girl inside her Victorian house being waited on hand and foot, who knew nothing about Shanty Town or life in the outback.

Nevel's thoughts were interrupted by a change in the atmosphere. Rustling sounds pervaded, and Nevel tried to convince himself it was just the wind. An owl hooted and Nevel felt shivers flash up his spine. Moments later, two mounted police came riding out of the shadows that loomed from the tall houses of town.

"Who goes there?" the police demanded as Nevel grabbed Quinn's hand and looked around frantically for a place to run. White picket fences stood in every possible escape path. There was nowhere to run.

"Is it one of the kids?" Nevel heard one policeman say to the other. "Quinn Dudley or Nevel Walker?"

Nevel looked at Quinn, but she kept looking straight ahead. Her breathing was no longer heavy. She looked regal, stoic. Nevel knew she was preparing herself for what lay ahead. Suddenly, the reality of the situation finally hit Nevel. They were caught. He would find out soon if he was brave enough to actually do what he had said he would do—to tell them he was indeed a bookkeeper to save Quinn. Nevel guessed she, too, planned to claim to be the book-keeper. They wouldn't believe him at first; she was the one pegged, but she wouldn't pass their tests. Still, how would he explain how he got his knowledge?

A booming voice shattered Nevel's thoughts. "Put your hands up, you're both under arrest under the sus-picion of treason."

24
Jail

Nevel had ridden a horse before, but never in handcuffs while being escorted by police. It was still pitch black out, and the darkness felt heavy on Nevel's shoulders. Turning the corner toward Government Square, Nevel was more scared now than he had ever been while running from Quinn or facing Driscoll. There was something very final about this leg of his journey. It would end, most likely, in the yard, where the gallows stood.

When they arrived at the station, Quinn and Nevel were left to shimmy off their saddles. Once they'd finally managed to reach the ground, the policeman grabbed them by their cuffed wrists and walked the prisoners into the station door. Nevel was behind Quinn, who walked as directed and kept her head down. She didn't fight or look back for reassurance from Nevel. They entered the station—moving closer towards their doom with every step—and he tried to wish it all away: being found out by Quinn; fleeing through the desert; discovering the depository; journeying home to say goodbye to his parents. Nevel had always known his story could end this bad, but Quinn had no business being hanged for his curse.

Inside, the station was lit by oil lamps, and several uniformed men sat at wooden desks with quills and ink beds and logs. Nevel noticed how clean everything was—the desks, the walls, and their uniforms. Nevel didn't see heroes in the starched black uniforms. Instead, he saw nothing but tattletales and brown-nosers, men who were driven by greed—not valor—and would stop at nothing to please Chief Commander Carrington. Real heroes are willing to get dirty, he thought to himself. Real heroes carried the stench of the dumping grounds, where they tried to clean up in order to protect the local ranches and farms. Real heroes had sweat on their brows from hours of work digging wells to keep their citizens healthy. Real heroes had blood on their hands carrying injured citizens to doctors in town. These policemen were not heroes; their hands were lily white and free of calluses that boasted hard work.

Nevel had heard the stories of these uniformed officers raiding gardens outside of town, claiming the crops were planted using stolen information. The same men took wool from the ranches and said it was a tax for use of the land. All of the goods taken from the hard-working citizens were given to Chief Commander Carrington and his local branch of government.

"We believe we got our fugitives," the policemen reported at the first desk as one of the seated men scribbled the information down in his log, the taller of the two speaking for both. "They match the descriptions for Nevel Walker and Quinn Dudley. One suspected bookkeeper, one harboring the fugitive." Nevel glanced around and saw three empty cells. He knew why they were empty. The government didn't waste a lot of time holding criminals these days. Hangings were far too entertaining in this world without TV or books.

"Throw 'em in B cell."

The officers grabbed Quinn and Nevel by the arms and pulled them towards the second cell–close enough for the officers to keep an eye on them, far enough away to allow the cops to talk without being heard, Nevel thought. As the steel bars rattled open, their handcuffs were removed and they were shoved into the cell. The metal clank that locked them inside with the slamming of the door felt like a punch to the gut to Nevel. His days of freedom were over.

Nevel wrapped his fists around the cold metal bars and watched as the uniformed men gathered around a desk. He could hear their muffled conversation, but they spoke too softly for him to make anything out. Behind him, he could hear Quinn pacing, but he could hardly face her.

"Well, this wasn't part of the plan." Quinn said complacently. He turned just as she slumped onto the cold cement bench. Even there, she was beautiful.

"I'm so sorry Quinn. This is all my fault." A cold sweat broke out down the back of Nevel's neck. He could accept his own death, but bearing the burden of her death would be too much. Quinn patted the bench next to her and tried to offer a smile, but Nevel could tell it was faked. "Quinn, I'm taking the fall here," he told her, silently pleading with her not to argue. "I am coming clean about everything. You ought to be released after they talk to me." Nevel was not able to look her in the face, so he stared at the ties on his boots as he approached her and sank down to sit next to her on the bench.

"Not a chance, Nevel." Quinn said with forced faith as she tapped her foot on the ground, looking at her toes, her elbows resting on her knees. "I'm going to tell them I am the bookkeeper. I am smart enough to string them along...for a while at least. It will buy us time." She lifted her head to look at Nevel and continued to speak quietly. "Driscoll will come when he finds out we're here. He'll get us both out—"

"He'll get you out, Quinn," Nevel cut her off. He was surprised to find he sounded calm, even as her pitch rose with every word.

"He knows I won't leave without you!" Quinn stood up, her voice louder now, and stomped in front of Nevel with her hands on her hips.

The group of policemen that had been gathered around the desk broke and the two who had marched them in now walked toward their cell. Nevel grabbed Quinn's hand and squeezed it twice. She squeezed back, hard. And then they let go.

"OK, Bookkeeper, time to chat," the taller police

officer said at the cell door, the shorter officer standing silently behind him with his hand on his gun.

Quinn and Nevel both stood up.

"I just want the girl," he barked as he unlocked the metal door with the key ring on his belt.

"Oh, I thought you said you wanted the bookkeeper," Nevel said, his voice dripping with sarcasm as he stepped forward.

Quinn immediately stepped forward as well, standing next to Nevel, her hand on Nevel's arm as if to push him back. "Well, here I am!"

"You know she is just trying to cover for me, I am the bookkeeper!" Nevel stated calmly, shaking off Quinn's grasp and stepping around her.

"I am the bookkeeper," Quinn calmly confirmed. She strode confidently past Nevel, and as she stopped in front of the lanky officer, Nevel was reminded again just how tall she was. She stood almost nose-to-nose with the leering man.

"I see," the lofty policeman said as he rolled his eyes. "Well, we'll start with Red here first." The shorter policeman yanked the cell door open at this cue and grabbed Quinn by the upper arm with unnecessary force as the taller policeman exited the cell. It made Nevel's skin crawl. He couldn't just watch them take her; he had to do something. As the shorter officer passed Nevel in the cell, dragging Quinn out, Nevel gathered all of the saliva in his mouth, pursed his lips, and spit at his face.

The policeman kept his tight grip around Quinn's arm—Nevel could see her skin turning white around his fingers—as he wiped the saliva from his cheek with the back of his other hand. His brown eyes narrowed on Nevel, and he pulled back his free hand and smacked Nevel so hard across the face that it sent Nevel flying across the cell only to land on his back on the cold cement. The taller officer intervened, hearing the commotion.

"Move on," he ordered to the shorter officer who looked down and walked out with Quinn still in his grip. The taller officer slammed and locked the cell door behind them.

Nevel's face stung like he had been attacked by a hive of bees. He blinked as his eye began to swell, and he watched helplessly as Quinn was marched down the hallway to a place where Nevel could not protect her. Three of the other policeman followed. An officer with glasses stayed behind, reclining back in a chair with his feet propped up on the desk, his eyes on Nevel.

25

Interrogation

Nevel paced the cement floor for what seemed to be hours. It was late, and he knew he should sleep to keep his mind keen when it was his turn to be interrogated, but the pit in his stomach wouldn't allow it. He was terrified for Quinn. He knew she would offer bits of her knowledge in between taunting, sarcastic bites that would surely enrage the officers; they would lash out at her insubordination. Nevel tried to blink away the images in his head of their lily-white hands on her throat, slapping her beautiful face, squeezing into fists that would fly at her jaw.

Nevel moved to the bars at the front of the cell and wrapped his fingers around them. He leaned against them, pressing his ear between the bars to listen. He couldn't hear anything—no talking, no doors slamming, no screaming—But Nevel wasn't reassured by this; he had read about soundproofed interrogation rooms in jails similar to this one. Beads of sweat surfaced on his forehead. He kicked the bars in front of him and began pacing again.

As more time passed, Nevel paced the cell frantically; his fists clenched at the thought of those despicable men laying their hands on Quinn. To them, she was a bookkeeper, another source of income and power to be sucked dry and used for personal greed and gain. The Australia that Nevel had been born into was no more; corruption was the name of the game now. He lay down on the cement bench, defeated, but he didn't sleep. His heart pounding, he simply waited with a lump in his throat.

Dawn began to break, and Nevel could see slices of pink and orange begin to dance through the jail windows, seeming to keep beat with his rapid pulse. Suddenly, he heard a door down the hall open. Nevel jumped to his feet and leapt to the front of his cell. He gripped the bars and craned his neck to try to catch a glimpse of Quinn. Instead, the same two officers that had taken Quinn away were walking out of the shadowed hallway and towards Nevel's cell.

"Where is she?" Nevel moved along the bars in his cell toward them. "What have you done with Quinn?" Nevel's tone bordered on hysteria. His hair was matted with nervous sweat. He moved, panicked, along the open bars to try to catch a glimpse of her, but to no avail.

"It's your turn now," said the stocky officer— in whose face Nevel had spit last night. The taller officer unlocked the cell door and the short officer grabbed Nevel by the upper arm. He squeezed so tight that Nevel could feel the pain all the way to his bone. Nevel's eyes darted about the hall, searching for some sign of Quinn—nothing.

The officer dragged him by the arm towards a door down the hall. Nevel deliberately lagged as he gathered information, forcing the officer to yank him by the arm to keep up. Nevel scanned the station as he walked, storing photographs in his mind of everything he saw— the number of doors he passed, which ones housed windows, the types of shoes the officers wore, the rip on the left pocket of the shorter officer's uniform, and the number of steps they took as they moved from the cell to the door—in case it could offer him an idea of escape once he found Quinn.

Passing through the door at the end of the hall, Nevel found at least a dozen more solid metal doors. The windowless doors were all closed, except for one halfway down the corridor, which was propped open by a cement block. The door was at least a foot thick, like a bank vault. The officer led him to the open room and followed Nevel inside, slamming the door behind him.

Inside was one wooden table with three chairs on one side and one chair on the other. The tall, beady-eyed officer closed the door as the short officer slammed Nevel into the chair that sat alone. Other officers, who had been waiting inside for him, took their seats across from Nevel.

The room had no windows and was the same sterile white and gray as the rest of the building. Two oil lamps were lit and were attached to the walls; one large candle flickered on the table. Nevel knew dawn was breaking, but in this room it could have just as well been midnight. Nevel felt like the walls were closing in on him. No matter where Nevel looked, all he saw was cement. This was like a coffin, a tomb. He imagined himself sucking in air from the cracks around the sealed door.

"You know, I owe you something," the stocky officer said with snakelike charm. He was so close that his sour breath was hot on Nevel's ear. As Nevel turned to face him, clueless to what the officer could possibly owe him, he was met with a wad of spit that hit him square in the eye. The slimy spray dripped from his eyebrow down his cheek. Nevel wiped his eye with the cuff of Driscoll's oversized shirt and rolled his eyes, refusing to give the officer the satisfaction of seeing him grimace in disgust.

"So you are Nevel Walker?" the tall man began as rounded the table. He turned a chair around and straddled it with a smirk.

"Yeah," Nevel grunted, already annoyed.

"And you claim to be a bookkeeper?"

"Yeah, that's right," Nevel confirmed. The short, stocky cop shook his head in disbelief, looking at the tall, beady-eyed one.

"And how is it that you have kept this from your government?"

Nevel rolled his eyes again. He wanted to laugh, but instead he replied, "It was easy. You people never asked."

The cops were visibly irritated by Nevel's candor

as they adjusted themselves in their chairs and leaned forward on the table with more intensity.

"When did you realize you were a bookkeeper?" The tall cop was clearly the interrogator, and the short stocky one, his muscle. The thin cop with glasses was acting as the transcriptionist, taking notes in an old logbook with a sharpened quill he continually blotted into an inkwell.

"When I was about six, I read the poem on the statue in town outside the library—it was '*For Australia*' by Henry Lawson—and I could see it like a picture in my head after that anytime I wanted," Nevel stated matter-of-factly and was quite pleased at himself with the story he now offered because he knew it was an example the officers could easily check.

"Can you recite that poem for us now?" The thin cop asked from over his logbook, clearly doubting that Nevel would be able to succeed.

Nevel cleared his throat, shut his eyes, and read to the policemen the first five stanzas of the poem in his head. When he was finished, he opened his eyes and looked right at the beady-eyed policeman, staring him down as he recited the final stanza:

"Books of science from every land, volumes on gunnery,

Practical teachers we have at hand, masters of chemistry.

Clear young heads that will sift and think in spite of authorities,

And brains that shall leap from invention's brink at the clash of factories.

Still be noble in peace or war, raise the national

spirit high;

And this be our watchword for evermore: "For Australia – till we die!"

The skinny officer was scribbling away as the other cops looked at each other in disbelief.

The beady-eyed cop lit a rolled cigarette and blew smoke at Nevel. "He isn't as stupid as he looks!" he said as he stood and walked around the table to Nevel, taking long draws from his cigarette. "But I could memorize that statue's poem if I wanted. Maybe he needs a reminder to quit lying to us about being the bookkeeper!" Looking at the stocky cop with a grin, he took his cigarette and held it between his thumb and index finger and stabbed Nevel on the hand with it—the same hand Quinn had cut in the desert. Nevel jumped, pulling his arm in to cradle it with the other. It burned on the spot, hitting his previous injury, sending a shooting pain that coursed all the way up his forearm. The cops laughed. He could smell his flesh and it made him queasy. He fought back the tears welling in his eyes. He took a deep breath and pulled *Great Expectations* from the library in his mind to try to distract himself from the pain.

The cops waited and Nevel knew he had to forge on, to prove he was indeed the bookkeeper. He had to offer more evidence.

"Suffering has been stronger than all other teaching, and has taught me to understand what your heart used to be. I have been bent and broken, but—I hope—into a better shape." Nevel looked the beady-eyed cop square in the eyes. "That was Charles Dickens' *Great Expectations*, Chapter 59, page 542."

"Anybody can pick up quotes on Brary Day," The shorter officer refuted, looking to the taller officer for approval.

"I'm going to ask you to recite specific passages and you are to respond immediately." The thin cop leaned down, fumbling with something under the table, and Nevel thought he heard a bag unzip. The officer sat back up and presented a thin notebook, clearly old and very battered. He pushed his glasses up his nose before looking at Nevel. Nevel worried for a moment that he might not know all the books; these men obviously didn't know how being a bookkeeper worked. The officer flipped through the pages and then glanced back at Nevel. "Charlotte Bronte's *Jane Eyre*, Chapter 23."

Thank God, Nevel thought, a fan of the classics.

Nevel kept his eyes locked on the men across from him. He was still shaken by the burn, but his blood boiled in anger at the thought of what they may be doing to Quinn, and he was ready to make them the fools. He spoke with clarity and maturity, both hands flat on the table now, burn and all.

"Do you think I am an automaton? — a machine without feelings? and can bear to have my morsel of bread snatched from my lips, and my drop of living water dashed from my cup? Do you think, because I am poor, obscure, plain, and little, I am soulless and heartless? You think wrong! — I have as much soul as you — and full as much heart! And if God had gifted me with some beauty and much wealth, I should have made it as hard for you to leave me, as it is now for me to leave you. I am not talking to you now through the medium of custom, conventionalities, nor even of mortal flesh: it is my spirit that addresses your spirit; just as if both had passed through the grave, and we stood at God's feet, equal — as we are!"

After more ink blotting and note-taking, the officer asked, "*The Grapes of Wrath*, page seventy-seven. Any line."

Nerves rattled as Nevel scanned for the book and came up empty-handed. "I...I..."

"Don't know that one?" the beady-eyed officer said, seeming pleased.

The scribe had set down his book and was scribbling notes in his log. After a few moments, he looked up and, with a quick flip through his notebook, prompted Nevel again. "*The Scarlet Letter*. Hawthorne. Chapter 11. The sentence begins 'Calm, gentle...'"

Nevel took a moment to find the book and passage and then answered with returned confidence. "Passionless, as he appeared, there was yet, we fear, a quiet depth of malice, hitherto latent, but active now..." Nevel trailed off, watching the beady-eyed cop pace, smoking a new cigarette now, while the stocky one stared and the logger took down notes and read from his book without looking up.

"Poe, 'The Sphinx'. The line begins 'Estimating the size of the creature—

"By comparison with the diameter of the large trees near which it passed—"

"Enough!" The beady-eyed cop slammed his fist on the table, leaning in towards Nevel with smoky breath. "How have you gotten all these books in your head?"

Nevel swallowed. "Brary Day—"

"No bloody way!" The beady-eyed cop slammed his fist again on the table. This time he grabbed Nevel by the hair and pulled him across the table. The cigarette dangled from his lip as he growled, "You think we're stupid, Bookkeeper? You calling me stupid?"

Pain shot from the roots of his hair. Nevel imagined the skin on his scalp would pull up soon.

"It was before the MegaCrash. I saw a lot of books when I was three." Nevel winced and hoped this lie would hold.

The cop let go of his hair, and Nevel sank back into his chair. Suddenly pain shot through his uninjured arm; the beady-eyed officer had stubbed out his cigarette on Nevel's right hand. It stung, and Nevel bit his lip to keep from crying out in pain.

The beady-eyed officer motioned for the others to go to the door. The officer with the log was still scribbling, and the tall officer smacked him on the back of the head to get his attention. No one spoke; the screeching of the chairs pushing away from the table as the officers rose and the clicking of their shiny heels on the cement floor were the only sounds that preceded the slamming of the heavy door. Silence fell and Nevel sat alone, his hands shaking from the pain of the burns, his heart aching for Quinn. He hoped he had given enough for them to release Quinn, even if it meant they would hang him in the end.

26

Sentencing

Nevel did not hear the footsteps that approached the windowless interrogation room. The sudden slamming open of the door and the instant flooding of light into the room startled him and knocked him out of his chair and onto the cold cement floor. A shiny black shoe kicked Nevel in the stomach, and Nevel groaned.

"Get up," the officer demanded.

Spots clouded his vision, and Nevel had to rub his eyes to see his tormentor. It was his tall, beady-eyed adversary. Nevel was relieved he was not smoking a cigarette.

"Up!" he was kicked again, and Nevel winced in pain while trying to get to his knees.

Beady-eyes yanked him up by the arm, and Nevel

was again in the hall, shuffling back towards his cell. In the corridor, Nevel still saw no sign of Quinn. He was confused when they passed his cell, walked right past the officers' desks, and went straight for the front door.

The short, stocky cop pushed the heavy door open. Nevel held a hand up to keep the glare of the sunlight from burning his retinas. Loud jeers from a huge crowd enveloped him. Suddenly, an officer from behind him was binding his wrists. He was pushed onward and soon the cement beneath his feet turned to dirt as he stepped outside. Slowly, he started to piece together what was happening. He had seen this before; sometimes he had stopped on his bike rides home from school when he would see a crowd gather outside of the jail. He would watch as prisoners were taken to the courthouse to receive sentencing.

"Traitor!" He heard a shout from a low-voiced man. "He's just a boy!" A woman in the crowd pleaded. There were dozens of people crowded outside the jail. The police officers on either side held Nevel tightly by the arms, but his head was free to search the crowd for familiar faces. He did not see Driscoll. This was unsettling as Nevel realized Driscoll was his only hope for escape. His eyes continued to scan until they landed on the stricken faces of his parents. His heart plummeted into his gut. Nevel could see tears streaming down his mother's face, and he imagined his father's eyes were pooled with water. They stood still among the gyrating protestors, their eyes locked on their son. Nevel tried to feign a smile, but he was withered and tired. The officer kicked

Nevel forward, forcing him to continue walking, and he lost sight of his parents in the crowd.

"Hang him! Hang him!" The mob's chanting rang in his ears. "Release him!" others shouted, but it was faint amongst the majority's condemning calls. His head felt light; his ears felt as though they were stuffed with cotton as he instinctively tried to drown out the harsh echoes of the crowd.

Nevel had nowhere to look but forward. It was hard to see much beyond the circling protestors and jeerers of the crowd that surrounded him. He wondered if Quinn had been released. His heart skipped a beat at the thought of her. More police officers joined them now to control the crowd that was hindering their walk to the courthouse. Nevel was bumped about as officers and citizens ebbed and flowed like currents in the undulating crowd. The ties were rubbing his wrists, and he could still feel the sting from the burns on his hand. His body ached from the beatings of the interrogation. His strides were monotonous; it was useless to try to do anything but follow protocol now. The addition of officers helped clear a path before him. About fifty feet ahead, there was another crowd and Nevel knew it could only be for one reason—Quinn was ahead of him about to receive her sentencing as well. His stomach twisted.

A tall, white picket fence surrounded the large brick courthouse; the single gate was manned by a dozen guards and stopped the crowds of protestors and onlookers in their tracks. Only prisoners and government were allowed beyond this point. As the sea of people ahead cleared, Nevel finally laid eyes on

Quinn.

She looked OK. Like him, she seemed tired and groggy, but he didn't see any marks of beating or torture—at least not from this distance. Nevel was relieved for a moment, but then fear began to well up again. He didn't see Driscoll in her crowd either. A big man like that would not have gone unnoticed. Nevel scanned left and right. He craned his neck forward and back over his shoulder. Driscoll was nowhere to be seen. Nevel could feel his shirt sticking to his sweaty back and he wished his hands were free so he could wipe the perspiration from his brow. Without Driscoll, there was no chance for them.

Nevel was guided up the tall brick staircase and past the looming white columns, to the arched mahogany doors of the courthouse. Inside, the air was sticky and thick. Nevel looked up. Rows and rows of heads filled the seats in the balconies overlooking the main floor. Morgan Creek's citizens must have waited all night to be allowed a seat in the hearing. He was escorted forward by the beady-eyed and stocky cops, past the mahogany pews filled with government types, women in big hats with lace embellishments and men with coats and bowties. They were always awarded the best seats for these types of events. Nevel was led to the first wooden pew on the left side of the courthouse and he watched as Quinn was lead to the first one on the right. At this moment, Quinn finally noticed Nevel, and forced wide smile. Her grin was quickly shaken as they were compelled to rise when the wigged judge entered the room. All turned to the great balcony overseeing the courthouse.

From behind royal blue velvet drapes came Chief Commander Carrington, escorted by his personal guards. Carrington was tall and well-groomed, his milky oval face framed by slick auburn hair. A handlebar moustache drew attention away from his pointed nose, and his small thin lips were tight in a straight line. He wore his military best, adorned with stars and pins and badges and stripes. The crowd cheered at the sight of him, but was quickly hushed as he held his right hand up high and then quickly clinched it into a fist. He sat in a throne of a chair and nodded to the judge. With that, the judge commanded all to be seated with his hands, palms pushing down.

"The case of Nevel Walker on the accusation of treasonous withholding of government services in respect to the gift of bookkeeping. What say you?"

The judge looked at Nevel first and the words leapt from Nevel's lips, "Guilty, your honor." His voice echoed, and the crowd seemed to gasp in unison.

The judge's eyes scanned to the other side of the room. "The case of Quinn Dudley on the accusation of treasonous withholding of government services in respect to the gift of bookkeeping. What say you?"

Don't do it, Quinn, Nevel thought, let me take the fall. He narrowed his eyes on Quinn, willing her to look at him, but it was futile; she stared straight ahead at the judge.

"Guilty, your honor," Quinn responded in a clear voice.

Nevel's heart sank; his gut twisted. The crowd broke into a thousand conversations.

The judge hammered his gavel. "Silence!" he bellowed. "Be seated."

Nevel sat on the pew between the two officers. Everything around him—the noises, the movements—seemed to spin into one continuous hum, and he felt like he was going to pass out.

"Before we call witnesses, I have a statement to read from the presiding officers who carried out thorough interrogations of both accused," the judge said. Nevel knew this was customary. Now they would find out if they passed the tests in their attempts to prove they were both bookkeepers. The judge cleared his throat and read in a booming voice. "Quinn Dudley did not prove herself to be a bookkeeper based on testing. Her trial continues under charges of fraud." The crowd gasped. Quinn shook her head no. Nevel felt some relief for her, but swallowed as the judge continued, "Nevel Walker did prove a possibility of being a bookkeeper based on testing." The crowd gasped again, and Nevel felt all eyes on him.

"We will continue the trial as planned with these facts in mind," the judge ordered as the room settled in for the drama to continue to unfold.

"First witness," called the judge.

Nevel looked up and saw his teacher, Mrs. Downey, approaching the stand. The spinning in Nevel's head stopped. He regained focus and watched as the trial proceeded.

A man in a suit began to pace. He spoke theoretically and in such an eloquent manner that it seemed to be more for the purpose of entertaining the crowd than to prosecute Nevel and Quinn. During the lawyer's soliloquy, Nevel rolled his eyes more than once. Nevel couldn't imagine when or how he would arrive at a point.

Finally, the lawyer approached Mrs. Downey. "What kind of a student is Mr. Walker?" he asked. He continued to pace as he awaited his answer as though he was deep in thought; Nevel thought it was simply to offer everyone in the room a view of his big part in this show.

"Terrible, really. He struggles. There's no way he could be—" Mrs. Downey's voice was shaky.

The man in the suit cut her off, and Mrs. Downey looked at Nevel with sorrowful eyes. "And Miss Dudley...what kind of a student is she?" The lawyer in the suit paced some more. Nevel swallowed hard; he prayed Mrs. Downey would lie.

"She is a hard worker. She does well, but I wouldn't say it comes naturally. I have had plenty of students who have done better—" Mrs. Downey was wringing the handkerchief she held in her fists. She looked at Quinn with pleading eyes, as if to ask for her forgiveness. Nevel was sure she was trying to cover for Quinn. He doubted she'd truly had better students. Nevel felt grateful for a fleeting moment.

"So Quinn is the smarter of the two!" concluded the lawyer in a large, bellowing voice that filled the room. "That is enough. Thank you."

No, that wasn't enough, Nevel thought. He looked around for more witnesses. The judge shuffled paperwork. The officers sat silently. "It isn't enough," Nevel wanted to shout it out as he looked around in a panic. Where were the other witnesses?

Just when Nevel had given up hope, it appeared someone was coming out of the witness door. Nevel couldn't see, but by the way the heads in the crowd were moving it seemed there was indeed another witness approaching. Nevel could begin to see a shorter person with black hair approach the stand. As he turned to take his seat, Nevel saw the freckles and bony elbows of Randy Thatchburne.

The lawyer began quizzing Randy on the actions of both Nevel and Quinn. "Quinn can memorize anything" was one comment he offered while, another was "Nevel doesn't even take notes". Nevel's skin crawled as he watched Randy enjoy the spotlight at their expense. Soon enough, Randy was excused and another witness was called.

Nevel was flush. All fingers were still pointing at Quinn, and he wondered if they thought she failed the tests on purpose. Driscoll was nowhere to be seen. Surely, he could have weaseled himself a spot in this courtroom with all of his connections. Nevel felt out of breath as he watched the open door from behind the judge's podium from which the witnesses were called forth. Through the crowd, all he could see at first was the top of someone's bowed head. And then he came into view. His normally strong, confident father walked out meekly with his chin tucked into his chest and his eyes on the floor. Holding his hat in his hands, Nevel's father sheepishly took the stand.

"My son is a good boy," his father spoke in a broken voice, as he seemed to make every attempt to stay in control of his emotions at the barrage of questions from the lawyer. "We live a simple life and have no idea how our son was brought into this situation."

"Why, then," the lawyer pried, leaning into the stand, "did your son...does your son claim to be a bookkeeper?" "What can I say?" his father replied. "He is in love, and young love knows no stupidity." The lawyer quickly excused Nevel's father. He looked to Nevel wistfully; Nevel knew he had done all that he could. He returned his father's stare with resolve and watched as a tear finally slid down his father's face as he was taken back out of the courtroom. "Final witness," called the judge and Nevel became hopeful again. Each prisoner had but one relative who could take the stand. He hoped that this would be when Driscoll would finally make his appearance and save Quinn. He looked to the witness stand and sat up in his pew as he waited for the final witness to surface.

A sharply dressed boy with jet-black hair and chunky cheeks, whom Nevel did not recognize, appeared. He looked to Quinn and saw her eyes rolling. It must have been one of her brother's, Nevel surmised.

The lawyer quizzed Quinn's brother about her intelligence and her access to books. The dumb brother told the court that he was sure she had been allowed in the library on days other than Brary Day, when her dad had to research a medical condition for one of the government folks. Nevel was irate as he watched Quinn's own brother ruin her. Nevel looked at Quinn and he could see the pain on her face. This was too much, even for a strong girl like her.

After another lengthy monologue, the sharply dressed lawyer closed his case and left it for the judge to decide.

The judge shuffled papers and nodded his head as officers and other courtroom staff whispered in his ears. The hush of the waiting crowd was riddled with whispers and finger pointing. Nevel looked at Quinn, but she did not look back; instead, she stared stoically straight ahead at the judge's bench. Finally, the whispers were hushed by the banging of the gavel. All eyes were on the judge as he gave the sentencing.

"It is a tricky situation in which both claim to be bookkeepers, hidden from the very government which has cared for and protected them—a government which does not deserve such treasonous acts!" The judge looked left and right as he spoke from his podium, and his voice echoed through the courthouse. His eyes narrowed on Nevel as he continued, "And only one of the accused can partially prove the possibility to have some bookkeeping capabilities." The judge's and the crowd's eyes now shifted to Quinn. "Still the other fits the mold, yet failed our tests." The judge looked up to Carrington and then back to the crowd at large. "As the evidence is not wholly convincing that either actually is a bookkeeper, and therefore can be of no use to the government in terms of intelligence gathering, we hang them both for this colossal waste of time and government resources!" Gasps ensued, followed by the gavel. "We shall hang them both in the yard tomorrow at noon!"

27

Last Rights

The march back to the jail from the courthouse was a somber one. The crowds still followed, this time cheering the capture and imminent execution of the traitors who had claimed to live in secret among them. Nevel was escorted by Beady-eyes and Stocky again, who were now heroes in the eyes of the towns-people as they hauled their traitor back to jail the night before his execution.

Nevel knew Quinn was somewhere ahead of him on her own march because he had watched her being escorted out of the courthouse before him. He prayed he would have a chance to see her and to speak to her once more.

Back inside the jail, Nevel was glad to be shel-tered from the jeering crowd. He welcomed the silence and was finally able to see more than three feet in front of him. Across the room, Nevel saw Quinn standing in the empty cell they had shared not long ago. She was combing her fingers through her long red hair and staring out the window with her back to him. She turned at the sound of the open door and looked at him. Neither one smiled.

"*Please take me to her*," Nevel silently wished as he was ushered towards the cells. Nevel held Quinn's stare with every step.

Nevel was escorted past the first empty cell, and then Beady-eyes reached for the keys to unlock the cell where Quinn was. His heart leapt. Nevel couldn't believe they would be given one last night together! As the heavy metal door slid open, Nevel rushed inside to Quinn. He wrapped his arms around her and she fell limp into his arms, nothing between them but their racing hearts. Nevel stroked her long hair, and she rested her cheek on his shoulder.

"Did they hurt you?" Nevel asked, knowing that the policemen were still watching.

"I'm OK," Quinn said, now wrapping her arms around him tight.

"Are you hurt?" Nevel asked, trying to pull her away a bit so he could get a look at her. He slid his hands along her long, freckled arms. He could see that Quinn did have red markings on her wrists, but so did he. Their restraints had rubbed them both raw. She leaned into him again. Nevel tried to pull her away to look at her face.

"No, I'm fine," Quinn said, reluctant to let go. Nevel stepped back. He now could see the beginnings of a black eye. Her lower lip was puffy, and the split was caked with dried blood. The blood in Nevel's veins rushed and he felt hatred well up inside him towards their keepers.

"Oh, God, they really hurt you," Nevel said as he cupped her face in his hand.

Quinn noticed the burn on his hand and she lightly glided over it with her thumb as she held his hand in hers. "Looks like they got you, too, Bookkeeper."

"I'm sorry they hurt you, Quinn, I—" Nevel started, but he didn't know what to say. He couldn't promise to protect her or keep her from harm's way. There was nothing he could do.

Nevel glared at the uniformed men beyond the bars of their cell. His fists clenched, and his blood coursed wildly through his veins in a boil. Quinn pushed the hair off his forehead.

"We've got bigger things to worry about," she whispered. "Did you see Driscoll in the crowd on the way to the sentencing?"

"No," he whispered back. His anger turning back to fear, Nevel turned and looked her in the face. "He wasn't there."

"He'll come through," Quinn said quietly. "We have nothing else to hope for."

A few moments passed. Nevel and Quinn held tight to their faith and each other.

"I'm not ready to die, Nevel," Quinn whispered and laid her head on his shoulder. Nevel grabbed her hand and kissed her forehead.

The front door to the jail opened, catching the attention of Quinn and Nevel. A tall, thin man walked slowly through the door. He was dressed in a black suit, with gray hair smoothed neatly back on his head. Quinn's body stiffened and straightened like an arrow.

The man approached the first police desk. His presence commanded their attention. He stated, "I am Dr. Dudley and I am here to see my daughter."

Quinn nervously began wringing her hands. Her eyes were darting everywhere but on her father. She smoothed the wrinkles in her dress with her hands.

"Chief Commander Carrington doesn't allow visitors after sentencing—" the officer with the glasses started to reply before Dr. Dudley cut him off.

"The only reason Chief Commander Carrington is alive is because of me! I demand to see my daughter!" Dr. Dudley ordered. Nevel was surprised to hear such power boom from such a small source, but he figured that desperation could give any manpower.

"Well, I—"

An officer with mousy brown hair and a pencil thin mustache appeared from the hallway and intervened. His uniform was neatly pressed; he looked like he was fresh. "Chief Commander has been expecting your arrival. I can authorize you to have a few moments in a holding cell with your daughter, out of respect for your services. Right this way."

Nevel remained on the bench while Quinn stood and walked sheepishly to the front of her cell.

"Dad." Quinn spoke in a trembling voice. She looked at her father through the bars and waited as the officer unlocked the cell and slid the door open. Quinn ran to him and wrapped her arms around him. Nevel knew from his talks with Quinn in the desert

218

that this was probably more love than had been showed between them in a long time, and his heart ached for them both.

"Quinn, my darling," Dr. Dudley cried, and they both sounded like they were sniffling between tears. They hugged for several moments until the mustached officer tapped Dr. Dudley on the back.

"Sir, we really must move on to another room," he said, and hurried them off to the interrogation room. Quinn and Dr. Dudley walked down the hall, arms wrapped tight around each other, until Nevel could see them no more. Nevel wished for a goodbye with his parents, but he had been given that before they were jailed. Plus, only someone of Quinn's stature in society could warrant a visit on the night before an execution.

Nevel paced his cell, scratching his head for ideas, to no avail. The room was empty except for Nevel and the officer with glasses that had logged his interrogation. Beady-eyes and Stocky were no doubt at a local pub by now, reveling in their heroism.

The sound of the front door of the jailhouse opening startled both Nevel and the officer at the desk. It was really late now, and the crowds from earlier had long subsided. The officer stood. Nevel walked to the front of his cell and wrapped his fists around the bars with his eyes on the door.

Nevel was shocked to see his father appear first, immediately followed by his mother. Unlike Dr. Dudley, at the sight of Nevel they rushed past the officer at the desk and straight to Nevel's cell.

"STOP!" the officer ordered. "You cannot just

barge in and—"

Still, the Walkers ran to Nevel as the officer in the glasses chased after them.

"Mum! Dad!" Nevel thought his heart would burst, his arms reaching through the bars to receive their hugs.

"Nevel, sweet Nevel!" His mother sobbed as she reached through the bars, completely ignoring the cop's order to back away.

"We are his parents," Mr. Walker pleaded. "We have a right to say goodbye to our son! You are going to kill him for no reason at all! You are going to put out a light in this world! Let us say goodbye at least!" Mr. Walker was in tears.

"I have strict orders not to allow visitors after sentencing." the officer tried to keep his calm, but his hand was on his holster, and Nevel could see his fingers twitching.

"But we couldn't see him before sentencing either! You turned us away!" His mother begged. Nevel imagined they had come several times while he had been in the dark solitary holding cell.

"Do you have a child?" Mrs. Walker asked through her tears, "It would be easier to die ourselves than to watch our child die! Please let us speak to him!"

This obviously struck a chord with the officer and he looked around the room. He was the only officer there—they all knew that—but he seemed to be double-checking.

"You got five minutes," the officer reluctantly gave in, and Nevel's parents rushed back to the cell.

They pulled Nevel into the tightest hug they possibly could around the prison bars.

"I have to tell you something," Nevel whispered to his dad while they hugged. "I hid the register."

"Did you scan it?" his father whispered back.

"Yes." Nevel said, hushed.

"We're going to get you out of here," Mr. Walker promised. "I don't know how, but we will. When you get out, there is an opening to the tunnels under the statue in front of the library. Drop down there and run until you reach a huge well pipe. I will meet you there." Nevel nodded and looked him in the eyes, but he knew he would never see the tunnels. His limp body would hang at noon.

"Nevel, I love you." Mrs. Walker whispered in his ear. "Have faith. This cannot be how your life ends. We will not stop until we figure out how to save you—" Nevel hugged his mother through the bars, but gave little credit to her words. There was no hope.

"Time's up!" The officer came towards the Walkers. They reluctantly let go of Nevel with tears streaming down their cheeks and were escorted out of the jail.

Nevel wiped the corners of his eyes where he felt pools of water threatening to spill and blinked until they dried again. Just a few moments later, Quinn appeared. She hugged Dr. Dudley, and her breaths were choppy from crying. He couldn't hear what she said to him or what Dr. Dudley said in return, but he could see the love between them. Dr. Dudley was escorted away quickly as Quinn was returned to her cell.

Inside Nevel grabbed her hand and they sat together in silence for a while. "You OK?" Nevel asked, knowing it was a stupid question. She was sitting on death row, waiting to be saved by her newly discovered outlaw of a father. On top of that, she had just said goodbye to the only father she had ever truly known.

"Yeah. You?"

"I'm OK. My parents came, too." Nevel whispered. "Dad told me how to get to the tunnels from here if we make it out."

"When we make it out," Quinn whispered back and smiled.

Nevel and Quinn sat up at the sound of the front door of the jail opening again. A short, plump man with a dark trench coat and hat entered. He held a black notebook, from which he seemed to be reading. He spoke quietly to the officer in glasses. He then looked to Nevel and Quinn and nodded to the officer. As dawn was breaking beyond the window, the man interrupted the quiet of the jail with his announcement, "Last rights!"

28

The Yard

The priest was looming in front of their cell, his hands on his bible and his eyes on Nevel and Quinn. "Do you wish to accept your last rites?" the portly man asked.

Nevel immediately replied, "Yes." He didn't notice that Quinn was silent and had backed away from the bars.

The priest placed his hands through the bars on Nevel's bowed head as he began to mumble words of prayer, "Blessed be God: Father, Son, and Holy Spirit."

Nevel felt anointed oil on his forehead and turned up his palms to receive it there as well. His heart pounded.

Suddenly, it was over. The priest and the tall cop

were walking away from the cell. Nevel turned to Quinn.

"But, you—" He didn't understand why she had turned them away.

She didn't have time to respond. The officers were all there now, in the cell, binding their hands and preparing to escort Nevel and Quinn to the yard.

"Let's go," Beady-eyes told Nevel as he grabbed his left arm and Stocky grabbed his right. Nevel looked over his shoulder toward Quinn. The officer with the mustache grabbed Quinn's right arm and the officer with the glasses grabbed her other. She was pulled out of the cell in front of him and she craned her neck to meet eyes with Nevel before she was jerked forward and forced to march out the front doors.

Outside, crowds had gathered again. Nevel's eyes scanned the mob, but everything was happening so fast today. He could not find a face he recognized. He was being pushed forward. As they walked, Nevel strained against the officers' tight grips to see Quinn. He saw flashes of her long red hair, which shone in the afternoon sun, but never her face or her tall, confident figure; too many officers obstructed Nevel's view. All he could see was her red hair along her back as she marched toward her death.

"Hang them!" The chant from the day before echoed again through the crowd. He searched the sea of angry faces, but Driscoll was nowhere to be seen. The crowd was one large sea pushing them toward the gallows.

"Traitors!" someone shouted.

Here and there, Nevel recognized the faces amongst the riotous mob—he was paraded past several of his haughty classmates, and Mrs. Thomas let out a particularly loud sob when he passed; Stocky swatted aside her flour-caked hands as she reached for him—but he didn't see his parents.

"They're innocent!" a woman screamed.

"Stop this witch hunt!" another woman's voice rang. Nevel wondered if it was Mrs. Downey.

"Kill them!" Nevel heard a child yell and he could feel it in his gut.

On they marched. Quinn was ahead, he knew, but the crowds prevented him from seeing her. He thought he heard drums pounding faster and faster; or was it the beating of his own heart?

They were getting closer now; Nevel couldn't see more than a few feet in front of him, but he was sure of this because the crowd that had been moving forward was beginning to yield and fall back.

The sun was high and bright; Nevel had to squint to see the looming gallows up ahead. He saw the platform and the nooses swinging in the breeze. Up ahead, Quinn was being escorted to the wooden steps. How had it come to this?

Panicked, Nevel scanned the crowd again, desperate for the site of a hulking figure in the shadows or a shock of red hair and ruddy cheeks framed by a red, bushy beard. He looked over his shoulder once, twice, three times, but he did not see Driscoll. Had he written them off since they willingly left him on the porch that night, never to return?

Nevel walked forward. With each step his feet felt

heavier, as if they were coated in cement. His throat was dry, and his heart was pounding in his chest.

He was at the stairs now. Quinn stood in front of her block, the noose hanging above her head. She looked like an angel in white.

Nevel's guards released him once he reached the top step. He was shoved forward—most likely by Beady-eyes—until he stood at his block. The crowd's cheers rang louder than ever, although occasionally, boos could be heard.

Nevel looked out at the crowd. From here he could see all of the faces. His eyes darted, searching for the burly man who might still offer them a chance at escape, but it was useless; Driscoll wasn't coming to save them. Nevel's scanning eyes fell on his parents. Two officers held them back as they attempted to run to the stage. Their faces were drenched with pain and hopelessness. It was too much. Nevel had to look away, and he turned his eyes up to the sky. The sun burned his retinas as it burnt away his tears, but it didn't matter now. He would die today.

The wigged judge, who had sentenced them, appeared on the stage before Nevel and then Quinn, looking each in the face and nodding in confirmation. Nevel turned to look at Quinn. She, too, was staring into the blazing noon sun. Perhaps she had seen Dr. Dudley in the crowd. Perhaps she, too, had realized Driscoll was not there. Her eyes were as dry as Nevel's, and he admired her strength and prayed for a miracle.

As the judge descended the stairs again, a masked executioner appeared, cloaked in a black robe. He wove his way through the guards and approached the front of the stage to the sound of cheers and gasps from the audience. At the executioner's nod, the policemen nudged Nevel and Quinn to step upon the blocks beneath the nooses. Nevel swallowed against the lump in his throat. The clouds seemed to be spinning. His head was fuzzy again. The cheers and shouts were muted by the pounding of his racing heart, which seemed to be about to burst through his chest. "Look to the moon, look to the sky," he told himself, but he didn't feel any calmer. The hands of the police escorts forced Nevel's head through the noose. The rough rope scratched his neck. He couldn't breathe. The executioner held up his hand; this was the signal. When he dropped his hand, the blocks would be kicked from beneath their feet, and Nevel and Quinn would hang.

Nevel took one last, long breath. He closed his eyes, overwhelmed by his racing thoughts. He was a fool to have ever trusted Driscoll. He was as bad as a murderer now since Quinn would hang for his crime. His death would crush his parents.

The executioner swung his hand down, but nothing happened. Nevel opened his eyes to see why the officers had hesitated. Over the heads of the crowd, Nevel saw a large plume of smoke rising from the distance. The townspeople were now facing the other direction, their backs to the gallows as they watched the smoke spiraling upwards. Nevel heard their mumblings, but couldn't make out the words. What were they saying? Something about the library?

Where was the executioner? The officers who had

just been at his side were now gone. Now he could hear the murmurs, "Fire! The library is on fire!"

The crowds were all rushing away from the yard now, moving as one towards the burning library. Nevel turned to look at Quinn, who was still standing alive and awaiting execution. Next Nevel whipped his head to the right. Over his shoulder, he saw the limp figures of the officers slumped on the wooden floor of the platform. Beady-eyes lay dead in a pool of his own blood, an arrow stuck in his heart. A few steps ahead, the executioner dangled halfway off the stage, his blood dripping over the edge.

People were screaming and running in all directions to escape the yard. Nevel frantically tried to make sense of it and then his eyes landed on Driscoll. The huge man stood in the center of the yard with his army of outlaws around him; the men all had weapons. Everywhere Nevel looked, cops lay dead, their bodies riddled with stab marks and arrow shafts. Driscoll motioned for them to run. Quinn withdrew the noose from her neck and ran to Nevel. He was so shocked, she had to take his neck out of the noose for him. She was pushing him and screaming something, but Nevel's head was spinning too wildly to understand. She slapped him, and the stinging in his cheek snapped him back to the moment.

"RUN!" she was screaming. They jumped from the platform and ran towards the library, following the panicked masses. Driscoll and his crew had disappeared into the crowd. Quinn held Nevel's hand tightly as they fought through the crowds, who were now all trying to get into the library, some to put out flames, others to loot.

Using the chaos as their cover, they slipped unnoticed between the townspeople and ran to the statue. Nevel pushed with all of his might on the cement figure, but nothing happened. He smelled smoke and heard shouting from the back of the library. There was no time. He moved to the opposite side. He was sweating and shaking as he leaned in with his shoulder and pushed with all of his strength. He felt it move slightly, and continued to push until slowly, it tilted up as if on a hinge. With Quinn's help, Nevel pushed the statue onto its side. Finally, they could see beneath it into a dark, muddy tunnel that resembled a pothole.

"Jump in!" Nevel shouted at Quinn, who was already doing so. Nevel slid his back around while still holding up the weight of the statue and slipped into the dark hole. Nevel felt himself slipping down the cool red clay like it were a slide at a park. He couldn't see anything but dirt walls stretching endlessly ahead as the statue above fell back down over the top of them and shut out the light.

29

Darkness Into Light

The darkness was so deep and rich, it was disorienting. Nevel reached out his hands to feel his way along the tunnel. The walls were curved, cold, and damp. Down, down, down he stumbled until he slipped on the wet stone floor and landed hard with a thud. Ahead he could hear movement; he told himself that it was just Quinn. He had watched her go in ahead of him, but still he was frightened. Too much had happened too quickly. He did not trust his own shadow anymore. Still, he knew he had to move toward the sound. When the tunnel ceiling lowered until he could no longer stand, he dropped to his hands and knees and crawled deeper into the dark narrow passage. At least the floor had leveled out, and he was no longer struggling to keep from slipping downwards. His palms and knees stuck in the cool mud as he moved.

"Nevel," he heard Quinn call, her voice echoing off the clay walls. He moved faster to reach her.

Up ahead, a faint light cut through the darkness. Nevel continued to crawl amidst the shadows that now painted the cave walls he passed. As he got closer and closer to the light, he could see Quinn. She was there in the light, waiting. Like an angel she knelt bathed in the faint light, and he could feel a warmth return to his heart. Nevel felt a rebirth of hope, of a future that moments ago had been all but extinguished.

She crawled to him, her white dress stained with mud, her red hair matted to her beautiful face. She was smiling from ear to ear, and Nevel couldn't help but smile back.

"Nevel!" She beamed, and they fumbled into a passionate hug in the dark, muddy tunnel beneath the library that surely still burned above. Nevel closed his eyes and tried to catch his breath. He fought to keep his heart in his chest. He could feel her heart pounding, too. He was shaking, still in shock. Quinn was warm, and the mud was cool, and Nevel was soaking in every sensation. He squeezed her tight and she nuzzled her face into his neck.

"I can't believe it," Nevel whispered.

"I know," Quinn replied.

They held each other tight. Finally, Nevel took a

deep breath and opened his eyes. It was time to figure out the next step. Still holding Quinn tightly, he surveyed the surroundings he could now see in the splinters of light. He saw a cylindrical stone structure behind Quinn that reached up through the mud ceiling above. The shards of warm light that peaked through the cracks in the stones were surely from the sun. This must be the well, Nevel thought. This was where his father had said he would meet him if they escaped. Nevel was in disbelief. Their journey would continue.

He pulled Quinn away to look at her. Nevel knew he was looking at his future. He wiped her matted hair from her face and cupped her cheeks in his hands. They were both still breathless from the run and the escape down the tunnel. Nevel kissed her forehead, pressing his lips hard against the skin, as if to make the kiss stick and stay forever. He slowly moved his face down until their eyes were locked and they were sharing the same breaths, and then he kissed her. They kissed as fast as they had run in the outback, as hard as the rock they had climbed. As Nevel kissed his Quinn, he could see flashes of scenes in his head of their adventures together. He saw her through the peephole in his door at home the day she showed up. He saw her leaning on the rock, where they had found their secret place. He saw her against the flames of the outback bonfires, her skin glowing pink in the flickering light.

Nevel pulled away when a subtle rustling sound stirred him.

"What was that?" Quinn asked.

Nevel pressed his finger to her lips to hush her. He

put himself in front of Quinn to shield her as he heard something coming toward them in the dark.

"Nevel, it's me," his dad said softly, and Nevel let go of the breath he had been holding.

"It's me, Nevel," his dad said again as he entered into the light where they could see him. He carried a backpack and had a look of sheer joy on his face.

"Dad!" Nevel crouched, standing as tall as the tunnel would allow, and moved to hug his father. His dad patted him on the back several times, muttering, "Thank God, Thank God," into Nevel's hair.

"We don't have a lot of time," his father said breathlessly. "I need to tell you how to go on from here before we lose our chance. You will become U.B.M. It's the best option. I'll spread the news that you both tried to get into the library and died in the fire; Driscoll will help me. You have to be dead to this town, or they will never stop searching for you. If you are U.B.M., we can stay in touch. We may even get to see each other again one day—" He paused; this comment seemed to affect him to the core.

"I brought a pack in case you made it this far." His dad stopped and looked Nevel in the eyes. Nevel knew his dad couldn't believe they were actually there. Neither of them had truly believed they would make it this far. "It has supplies and some books for trade. You'll need to get out of the local tunnels so you don't run into any U.B.M. members who are going to think you are dead by the morning." Nevel squeezed Quinn's hand and pulled her into his side as she smiled at his father. Hope was restored in Nevel's soul as he listened to the instructions.

"Follow the tunnel that way to the old mining pipe." His father continued. "This is where you can get out; you will be safe then. I am the only U.B.M. in this area that goes that far. On the other side of town, U.B.M. members will only know you as carriers. All carriers are strangers. You will need the pass of the crow. I have given you each one.

"There is a train station not far from here. A U.B.M. member by the name of Claude—their names are sewn right on their shirts—works there as a ticket-taker. Show him the pass of the crow, and he'll let you on. Take the train to Brisbane." Nevel nodded and took a deep breath. His father was talking fast. Every now and then he would wipe the sweat from his forehead. Nevel knew they had little time and that his father would have to make it back to town soon before anyone noticed he was gone.

"In this pack is a change of clothes for you both." Mr. Walker held the pack out to Nevel, who slung it over his shoulder. "You will need to appear clean to blend in with the higher ups on the train. Once you are in public places, you must blend in as tourists, visiting relatives—whatever you have to do. You've made it this far; you two are obviously strong together. If ever you need us, send word via the U.B.M. Use code and pseudonyms; we'll figure it out."

"OK, Dad, I got it." Nevel knew his father didn't want to leave. He tried to reassure him with a steady look.

"I know you do, son" Nevel's dad replied. "I know you do."

Nevel hugged his dad tightly, like he had when he

was little and scared of the dark. When they parted, he turned to go, with Quinn's hand clasped in his.

"I love you, son. I'll see you—" his dad seemed to be getting choked up as he turned to go the opposite direction.

"I love you, too, Dad," Nevel said, feeling his adrenaline beginning to kick back in. "We'll be in touch. I'll make you proud, I promise."

"I know you will."

Distant voices echoed through the tunnel, and Nevel's dad pointed for Nevel and Quinn to run before taking off in the opposite direction.

30

Ticket to Ride

Nevel and Quinn blindly ran for several long, muddy, dark miles, crouching to keep from hitting the low ceiling. When light began to shine ahead, Nevel knew they must be close.

"I think I see the pipe," Quinn said. Moments later, they reached the rusty brown conduit, which was surrounded by light from the space where it broke through the earth above. Nevel boosted Quinn up onto the pipe and she began to climb it to the surface. Nevel followed. There were plenty of large bolts to step on and grab, so the climb was not challenging. There was enough space for a body to generously move up it and onto the ground above. The opening from the tunnels came right out from behind an abandoned factory. The light was blinding after the darkness of the tunnels.

"We gotta get cleaned up and changed," Nevel said as he took in their new surroundings. Quinn nodded, panting to catch her breath. They scrambled around a puddle, dipping hands in to wash the mud and sweat from their faces and the dirt from their hands. Nevel tore off his shirt and replaced it with the fresh collared shirt in the pack. He motioned for Quinn to duck behind a piece of factory wall to change into the short navy dress he tossed to her. While Quinn was changing, Nevel pulled on his pants, glad to have clothes that fit again. He was lacing up his boots when Quinn emerged from behind the wall.

"You look—" Nevel lost his words as he laid eyes on Quinn. She looked beautiful, older somehow, like a woman instead of a girl.

"Yeah, you, too—let's go!" Quinn was pointing at the train station.

Nevel wasn't sure how far they would have to travel unseen, and was glad to see the green tin roof of the train station right across the street when they rounded the factory and reached the main road. Quinn and Nevel quickly approached a small crowd of people who stood around the cement platform with suitcases and fancy hats. There was a chatter that buzzed in the excitement of the train's impending arrival. Nevel and Quinn were easily able to slip right into the midst of the crowd.

A little girl, who must have been seven, tugged at her mother's dress. She had a blond doll under her arm that looked just like her, braids and all. Her mother was chatting with another woman about whether or not they would have dinner prepared when they arrived that night. "Mumsie, I want to ride the train. Mumsie, where is the train?" the little girl repeated over and over while her mother ignored her.

Another family stood to their left. The father was scribbling in his log, careful that no one could see. His son bounced a ball against the brick wall, and his wife was constantly primping her daughter, wiping the pleats on her collar and smoothing her hair.

Quinn and Nevel stood holding hands. Nevel was glad that no one cared to notice them in the crowd. This was good; they blended in well enough. After only a minute or two, a loud rumble began to surface. It shook the ground and reverberated in Nevel's chest. The train was coming.

The excitement was contagious; people on the platform cheered. The chugging grew louder and louder as the train neared the station. The cheers were drowned out as a black engine came speeding into view and screeched to a halt.

Relief spread all over Nevel's body when he saw a man with a nametag that read "Claude" appear from the passenger car. Claude stepped out on to the platform and held open the car door, calling, "ALL ABOARD!"

Quinn squeezed Nevel's hand twice. It was exciting to be sixteen and sneaking on a train with wealthy, important people. They followed the herd moving toward the car. When they reached Claude, they locked eyes but didn't dare acknowledge each other. Handing him their passes of the crow, which were quickly returned to them, Nevel and Quinn boarded the train.

Many of the adults turned right towards the dining car. The children—some with their nannies— went left to the traveling car. Nevel and Quinn followed the little girl from the platform into the traveling car to find a seat. The aisle of the car was a blue velvet carpet that matched the blue velvet seats. The curtains that framed the windows were the same blue velvet. At the end of the car were two empty seats. Quinn and Nevel quickly took them and sat in relief. "Whew," Nevel whispered into Quinn's ear.

"I think I held my breath for the last twenty minutes," Quinn whispered back.

In another moment, the whistle blew and a slow chug-chug-chugging eventually grew to a steady pace. Nevel's eyes were glued to the window. He'd never been on a train; never even left Morgan Creek for more than the car trips to his grandparents' house when he was little. He wanted to soak in every image to keep in his mind for later.

A door slid open in front of them. It was a man in a blue suit and polished hat. Clearly, he worked on the train. Quinn and Nevel grabbed hands as he walked up and down the aisles, punching tickets.

When the man stopped at Nevel and Quinn's row of seats, sweat began to bead at Nevel's forehead. "Tickets, please," the man asked without a smile. Nevel panicked. He had given their passes of the crow to Claude, who had returned them without question. Nevel hadn't realized that everyone else still held tickets.

"Sorry, sir. I believe my mum has them up in the dining cart," Nevel was quick to react. Quinn just smiled nervously.

"Right, well, what's her name? I'll go and ask her," the man didn't seem to be letting up. Nevel squirmed. He looked for Claude, but he was nowhere to be found.

"Oh, I have them, remember?" Quinn chimed in cheerfully and she started searching in the pack. Nevel tried to act naturally.

He worried how long this would take and what in the world she planned on pulling out to replace the ticket. He tried to make small talk in the meantime to help Quinn stall.

"Beautiful mornin', sir!" Nevel said.

"Mmm," the man grunted in return. His mustache was furrowed like his disapproving eyebrows, and he seemed to be quickly losing patience.

"I slept like a baby last night." Nevel tried. "What a refreshing morning! Can't wait to make it to Brisbane! Sleep well, last night, sir?"

"Crow kept me up," the man grunted, still annoyed. Nevel hoped this was not a coincidence. He hoped it was a sign—the sign of the crow. Nevel pulled out the two Pass of the Crow cards from his pocket and handed it to the man in lieu of the tickets, swallowing hard as the man took them. It was risky, but after his comment about the crow keeping him up, he hoped it would work.

The man stared at the two for a moment without speaking.

"Hmm," the man seemed baffled, looking at the two of them, then back at the cards. Maybe he had made a mistake, Nevel worried. Maybe he wasn't

U.B.M.; maybe it was a coincidence. The man passed the cards back, though, and quickly went on about his job without saying another word to Nevel and Quinn.

"It worked!" Quinn whispered in excitement. "I can't believe it!" Nevel whispered back. They could hear the man continue from seat to seat. "Tickets, please." His voice grew faint as he reached the end of the car. Breathing deeply in relief, Nevel turned back to watch the scenery out the window. Reds and oranges and the occasional greens flashed by in the landscape. Kangaroos hopped, and koalas hung from their eucalyptus trees. Nevel's pride for his country swelled in his heart. He was maintaining pieces of history. He was doing a service for his people.

"So what do you think?" Quinn snapped him out of his nostalgic trance.

"About what?" Nevel asked, trying to refocus.

"Where do we go when we get to Brisbane?" Quinn's wheels were clearly turning to piece together the puzzle in her mind.

"Oh, uh...I dunno—" Nevel was spellbound by the rocking of the train and the synchronized sounds of the chugging wheels. He couldn't focus; he was still trying to recover from his brush with death.

"I mean, I suppose we will..." Nevel said. As he began to strand together a thoughtful response to Quinn's questioning, she placed her hand on his leg to stop him.

"Nevel," she whispered. Nevel looked at her face. It was pale, void of her usual color and spirit.

"What is it," he asked. He followed the trail of her

green eyes to the door that separated their car from another.

On the glass, which was foggy from steam, a message was written: "TAKE THE R TO SEA. PORT OF CALL B."

"The R?" Quinn said, clearly confused.

"The Register," Nevel whispered, quietly and close to Quinn's ear, "It is THE book to the U.B.M.; the alpha and the omega, the beginning and the end, the one book that keeps the U.B.M. working—" "How do you know?" Quinn looked puzzled. "Because I took it from the depository. I read it before I gave it to my dad." Nevel was replaying the scene in his mind, his goodbye to Tank, his passing off of the Register through the sliding glass door.

"Well, what are we supposed to do?" Quinn asked while Nevel remained lost in thought. "I guess the U.B.M. thinks we have it. They're expecting us to take it to this Port of Call?"

Nevel paused and pushed his hair off of his head. "I don't know."

Silence pervaded as the train rocked gently along the tracks.

"So we head to The Gold Coast." Quinn seemed to be trying to lighten the mood. "I used to summer there. Have you been?"

"I've never even seen the ocean," Nevel replied.

The rocking of the train lulled them into silence. Giggles arose from the children playing dolls a few seats ahead of them. Cries from babies were shushed by their rocking Nannies.

Nevel looked out the window, wondering if their

high school class had held a memorial service upon hearing of their deaths. He imagined his dog, Tank, waiting on his front porch for him, to no avail. It broke his heart to know that Tank would probably wait for him there on that front porch forever.

Quinn was gazing out the window, too. Nevel knew she was probably imagining how life was back home as well. Did she miss Dr. Dudley? Did she wonder about her how life had been when she was a toddler, living as Driscoll's little girl? Nevel realized he didn't even know if she had a pet that she missed like he was missing Tank.

There was so much they knew about each other— the deepest secrets—but there was still a lot they did not know. This was Nevel's first train ride, but Quinn had summered on the Gold Coast with her family years ago. Was she remembering train rides with them? Were her thoughts of the happy, rich life before her mother died, when her adopted family loved her irrevocably? Was she wishing away the life she had chosen with Nevel?

Nevel took Quinn's hand, and she turned to him and smiled. They were in this together. Whatever lay ahead, they could handle. What was behind them had bettered them. The reds and oranges outside the train window began to fade into the dark of the night as they rocked and jerked down the Australian railway.

"Nevel," Quinn said curiously. She looked at him with the sly, challenging green eyes he knew from his days as her hostage in the desert. "If you have never seen the ocean, and I didn't see a swimming pool anywhere in your back yard...well...is it quite possible that you don't, in fact, know how to swim?"

"Not a bit," he said with a grin, amazed that their thoughts of survival were now watered down to small talk. But the light moment turned as a realization overcame Nevel. In the pit of Nevel's stomach, an unsettling feeling grew. He began to think about what purpose he would serve in the future for the U.B.M. and he realized he had not checked his pack. Did it contain anything that would put them in danger?

He opened the pack and shuffled through it. He hadn't taken the time yet to really look at what was inside. Buried beneath their soiled clothes, meager rations, and small stash of books Nevel's dad had provided, Nevel felt the leather of a hand bound journal. He pulled it out, careful not to let the other passengers see. It was the Register. He quickly pushed it back under their supplies. When Quinn raised her eyebrow in question, he shook his head.

"Your Pride and Prejudice gave me a paper cut," he said, and she rolled her eyes, but seemed satisfied. Quinn took the pack from his hands and set it on the floor at their feet. She leaned closer to him and rested her head on his shoulder, drifting into an easy doze.

Nevel thought he was going to be sick. He was still processing it all. Now that he held the Register, he felt a target reappear on his back.

When the train screeched to a halt a few hours later, Nevel and Quinn disembarked onto a crowded platform, where they quickly and purposefully blended in with the moving crowd. They walked, hand-in-hand toward Brisbane, Nevel carrying the weight of the world on his back.

ACKNOWLEDGEMENTS

Not a word to write would come to my mind if I did not receive the fuel of my writing which is the love of my family. I want to thank my **husband** for working hard to build a life for our family, for keeping me laughing, and for being my best friend. I love life with you. I want to thank my son, **Thomas**, for inspiring me to be more adventurous in my writing and for giving me survival tips. I want to thank my daughter, **Eliza**, for inspiring me to write a character who can be beautiful but still just as tough as a boy. Thank you both for your patience with me as writing sometimes interfered with playtime. May this book be proof to you both that hard work makes dreams come true. I love you to pieces. A special thanks to **Mom**, **Dad**, **Lindsey**, and **Britt** who encouraged me to write even from a very young age and who never stopped believing in me – I love you always; thanks to my **in-laws** for their love and support; thanks to my **aunts**, **uncles**, **cousins**, **nieces**, **nephews**, and **friends** for their support and help in promoting this book. What a blessing family is! My cup runneth over.

Lastly, I want to thank the **readers**. I hope you enjoy reading IAC as much as I enjoyed writing it.

ABOUT THE AUTHOR

Whitney L. Grady grew up in Warrenton, Virginia before leaving for college in North Carolina. She now lives in Kinston, North Carolina with her husband, two children, two dogs, and two cats. Whitney is a graduate of The University of North Carolina at Chapel Hill where she received a B.A. in English and East Carolina University where she received her Master's Degree in Education. This is her debut novel. For updates on book signings and appearances, visit www.whitneylgrady.com.

A Message From the Author:

Thank you for taking the time to read my book. I would be honored if you would consider leaving a review for it on *Amazon*.

Check out these titles from
Amazing Things Press

Keeper of the Mountain by Nshan Erganian

Rare Blood Sect by Robert L. Justus

Evoloving by James Fly

Survival In the Kitchen by Sharon Boyle

Stop Beating the Dead Horse by Julie L. Casey

In Daddy's Hands by Julie L. Casey

How I Became a Teenage Survivalist by Julie L. Casey

Time Lost: Teenage Survivalist II by Julie L. Casey

Starlings by Jeff Foster

MariKay's Rainbow by Marilyn Weimer

Convolutions by Vashti Daise

Seeking the Green Flash by Lanny Daise

Nikki's Heart by Nona j. Moss

Nightmares or Memories by Nona j. Moss

Thought Control by Robert L. Justus

Palightte by James Fly

I, Eugenius by Larry W. Anderson

Tales From Beneath the Crypt by Megan Marie

Vintage Mysteries by Megan Marie

Defenders of Holt by Julie L. Casey

A Thin Strip of Green by Vashti Daise

Fun Activities to Help Little Ones Talk by Kathy Blair

Trade of the Tricks: The Tricks' Brand by David Noe

Tears and Prayers by Harold W. "Doc" Arnett

Thoughts of Mine by Thomas Kirschner

Pass of the Crow by Whitney L. Grady

Check out these children's titles from
Amazing Things Press

The Boy Who Loved the Sky by Donna E. Hart
Terreben by Donna E. Hart
Sherry Strawberry's Clubhouse by Donna E. Hart
Finally Fall by Donna E. Hart
Thankful for Thanksgiving by Donna E. Hart
Make Room for Maggie by Donna E. Hart
Toddler Tales by Kathy Blair
A Cat Named Phyl by Donna E. Hart
Geography Studies With Animal Buddies by Vashti Daise
The Princess and the Pink Dragon by Thomas Kirschner
Sherry Strawberry's Coloring and Activity Book by Donna E. Hart
The Happy Butterfly by Donna E. Hart
From Seanna by Vashti Daise
The Boy Who Had Nine Cats by Irene Alexander
Meet Mr. Wiggles by Shivonne Jean Hancock
From Seanna Coloring Book by Vashti Daise

Amazing Things Press

www.amazingthingspress.com

37732538R00145

Made in the USA
Middletown, DE
05 December 2016